GUNS OF OCTOBER

A Brittle and Ashe Adventure

GUNS OF OCTOBER

by Timothy Friend

A Brittle and Ashe Adventure

Published by BAM Books

BAM Books
Kansas City, MO
USA

www.bam-books.com

ISBN: 978-17359805-2-2 (print)
ISBN: 978-1-7359805-3-9 (ebook)

For Jenn-
Rain or shine.

ONE

Of all the occupations Charlie Brittle and I had tried over the years, it was man-hunting that suited us best.

We'd only been bounty-hunters for a short time, but had proven to be naturals at it. The only problem we had was our differing views on how to interpret the decree 'Wanted: Dead or Alive'. The way I read it, the choice was an offer you made to the fugitive- surrender, or face the gun. To Charlie's way of thinking, if the law really wanted their man alive they would have put that part first.

We solved the matter by alternating our approach. Charlie's approach didn't amount to much more than walking up and shooting a man, often in front of a group of shocked and suddenly skittish onlookers. Times like that, it fell on me to show the paper we had on the dead man, settle everyone's nerves before more shooting broke out. I sometimes suspected that Charlie enjoyed the drama of it all and wouldn't have minded a little more shooting if it came to that.

I'd like to say there was less killing when we did things my way and announced ourselves and our intentions proper like. There wasn't. The men we pursued were mean, vicious, short-sighted sonbitches who could not foresee things going badly for them. Inevitably they would make their play, and we would shoot them dead.

This never bothered Charlie, but I found it so disheartening I was ready to go back to running our saloon, if not for the fact that it had been burned to the ground, and we hadn't made any money at it in the first place. Just about the time I'd given up on the notion of collecting a bounty on someone we hadn't first filled full of holes, we met Fat-Boy Barker.

Fat-Boy, along with his partner in murder and thievery Jimmy Thistle, had robbed a stagecoach and killed two passengers in the process before lighting out for East Texas. Charlie and I picked up their trail in Beaumont and followed their path along the Sabine River. I kept getting the nagging feeling that we were being followed, and I told Charlie about it.

Charlie said, "We know Fat-Boy and Jimmy are ahead of us, so what's your worry."

"My worry," I said, "Is whoever's behind us."

"That would be nobody."

I said, "I'm telling you, Charlie, ever since we left Beaumont, whenever I look behind me I get the feeling like somebody just stepped out of sight. Why do you think that is?"

After thinking it over for a minute, Charlie said, "I don't believe there's anybody back there, but I can see you're convinced. What do you want to do?"

I said, "Nothing I guess. You're probably right."

Charlie said, "Don't agree just to get along. I don't want to hear any 'I told you so' if I'm wrong."

"Oh, you'll for sure be hearing that. If it turns out I picked up on somebody following us before the great Charlie Brittle, you'll be hearing 'I told you so' for the rest of your born days. On my deathbed I'll be saying, 'I told you so.'"

Charlie said, "On your deathbed? So you plan on dying before me?"

I said, "Maybe I'm old and dotty and just forgot that you died already. Probably in some embarrassing and dishonorable way that pains me to think about."

Charlie nodded, said, "I can see that."

Eventually Fat-Boy's trail left the main road and followed a less travelled path that led Charlie and me into dense woods. Even with Charlie's belief to the contrary, I still had the sense that somebody was behind us, dogging our every step.

Despite the healthy lead they had on us, it seemed as if we were gaining on Fat-Boy and his partner with relative ease. It wasn't long before we found tracks that appeared no more than a day old. It was like they didn't care they were being pursued. Wasn't until we caught up with them that it finally made sense to me.

It was early morning when we found our men near the river. After spotting their tracks, Charlie and I decided to tie off our horses and pack mule and creep up on foot, the better to catch them by surprise. We found their camp and the two of us crouched in the brush to look things over. I spotted Jimmy Thistle sleeping soundly by a smoldering campfire, and snoring loud as a rockslide. It looked like a horse was laying on the ground beside him draped in a blanket, but when I saw both their horses tied to a nearby tree I realized I was mistaken.

I said, "That big heap there, covered in the dirty blanket?"

Charlie said, "Fat-Boy."

"Damn. No wonder they were so slow-travelling."

Charlie said, "He's a big boy all right. You still want to do it your way, Owen? We could just shoot'em both right here and be perfectly within the law."

"You can't be serious. Even you wouldn't shoot a couple of fellas in their sleep."

Charlie said, "Nah. First I'd yell something like, 'Wake up boys, it's judgement day.' Then I'd shoot'em."

I shook my head, said, "Sometimes you scare me."

"Your desire to palaver with men who want us dead don't exactly do my heart good."

"Fair point. But these boys are asleep, so this should go better."

"It'll go different," Charlie said. "Not so sure it'll be better."

We stood up then and stepped from the brush into the clearing. Charlie had one of his Colts in hand, the hammer thumbed back. I carried my .10 gauge cradled in my arms. I carried a Colt on my hip like Charlie, but it was mostly for show, as I was a terrible shot. The shotgun, a keepsake from my days riding for Wells Fargo, compensated for my lack of marksmanship. I had a second one back with my horse. I often carried it in a scabbered on my back, but had learned from experience that it was a hindrance when creeping around in thick woods.

True to his word, as we approached the sleeping men Charlie yelled, "Wake up, boys. Judgment day has arrived."

Neither man stirred. Jimmy's snoring carried on, loud and steady.

I said, "I'm guessing that's not the reaction you expected."

Charlie gave me a sour look. Then he said, "Get up, you sidewinders. The wrath of justice is upon you."

Jimmy smacked his lips, shifted a little there on the hard ground, then his snoring escalated from rockslide to full-on avalanche.

Charlie said, "Lazy sonbitches are spoiling my entrance." Then he fired his gun in the air.

Jimmy bolted upright, his head craning this way and that, his bug-eyes trying to see everywhere at once. Fat-Boy woke just as quickly, but it took a considerable amount of time and effort for him to work himself into a sitting position. When he saw Charlie and me, our guns aimed at him, his big shoulders drooped.

Fat-Boy said, "I never should have come to Texas."

I said, "We aim to take you boys back to Beaumont,

turn you over to the law. The only decision you have to make is how many new holes you want to arrive with."

Jimmy said, "None for me, thanks. I don't expect Fat-Boy here wants any either."

Fat-Boy said, "I can speak for my own damn self."

I said, "Yeah? So what's it going to be."

Fat-Boy craned his neck to look at me. His face was round and jowly, his eyes so deep set they were just black dots. When he spoke it sounded like the words were being throttled by the rolls of fat around his neck.

He sighed, said, "I don't want no new holes either."

Jimmy said, "All you did was tell'em what I already told'em."

Fat-Boy said, "Shut up."

"All I'm saying is, you make a big deal out of me speaking for you and then you go and say the same thing I did."

Fat-Boy said, "And all I'm saying is shut up."

Charlie looked at me, said, "Can I shoot'em now?"

Jimmy put both his hands in the air, said, "We done surrendered. No need to shoot nobody."

I said, "Put your hands down and stand up. Nobody's going to shoot you long as you move slow and easy."

Jimmy lowered his hands and stood up. "Only way I can move. Sleeping on the goddamn ground has me so stiff I can hardly stand up straight."

Charlie said, "I don't care if you stay bent at the waist. Just unfasten that gun belt and leave it on the ground."

Jimmy unbuckled his belt and let it drop. He kept on complaining. "I'm not cut out for sleeping rough. Goddamn chiggers are eating me alive. Only food we got is beans. And let me tell you, you don't want to travel downwind of Fat-Boy if beans is all you got on the menu. I'm so sick of smelling farts and sleeping in the woods, if I'd known you were looking for us I would have come found you."

Charlie waved his gun at Fat-Boy, said, "You too, big fella."

After working at it some Fat-Boy got to his feet. His big belly hung down and covered his belt buckle and it took a good deal of hoisting for him to undo it. I could tell it was making Charlie nervous watching the man's hand move around so close to his gun. I expected him to say the hell with it and shoot Fat-Boy, but despite his unease Charlie showed restraint.

Fat-Boy stared down at his gun belt when it hit the ground, said again, "I never should have come to Texas."

Jimmy said, "It's a long ride back to Beaumont. What kind of grub you boys carrying."

I hesitated before saying, "Mostly beans."

Jimmy looked like he was about to cry, said, "Shit. You fellas mind if I check my line?"

He pointed toward the riverbank where a piece of twine hung from a tree branch down into the water. The line was pulled tight, and it moved ever so slightly as I watched it.

Jimmy said, "I strung it last night, hoped we might

catch a fish for breakfast. Maybe a snapping turtle. Hell, even an old boot would be better than more beans."

Jimmy didn't wait for either Charlie or I to give the ok, just walked over to the tree and leaned out to grab the line. The twine was pulled out at an angle, making it difficult to reach from shore. Jimmy grabbed an overhead branch with one hand and reached out with the other far as he could, stretching himself out over the water.

He kept up a steady patter. "Looks like I might have caught something. I'll share it with you boys if you like. I can cook up a catfish will bring tears to your eyes."

There was an old log just under the surface of the water, and I saw Jimmy's foot come down on it as he struggled to get enough reach to grab the twine. The log shifted, and I expected it to roll out from under his foot at any moment and drop Jimmy in the river.

Jimmy was still telling us about his skill at cooking catfish. "My old gramma taught me how to do it up right. The most important thing to remember when you cook a catfish is-"

I never learned the secret to cooking catfish, because right then there was an explosion of water and mud and sharp teeth, and all at once an alligator clamped its jaws around Jimmy Thistle's head

TWO

After the gator latched onto Jimmy's head he lost his grip on the tree branch and fell into the mud. The gator thrashed around with Jimmy yelling up a storm. I can only guess that he was yelling for help because the actual words were muffled on account of his head being inside a goddamn alligator's mouth. He was still yelling when the gator slid off the riverbank and under the water, turning Jimmy's cries into bubbles. I watched the heels of his boots glide along just above the surface, his spurs glinting in the sun as the gator carried him out to deeper water.

I looked at Charlie and he looked at me, then we both looked at Fat-Boy, whose tiny eyes were widened in shock. None of us moved.

Charlie motioned toward my .10 gauge, said, "Shoot that thing."

I said, "It's out of range."

Charlie said, "Get closer. That's fifteen hundred dollars floating away."

We both looked out at the river. We still didn't move. Jimmy's bootheels disappeared suddenly, pulled down to the muddy river-bottom along with the rest of him.

A few ripples briefly marked his watery grave, then dispersed, leaving the river's surface smooth and glassy.

Fat-Boy said, "You just let him get eat."

Charlie said, "I didn't see you rushing to help."

Fat-Boy said, "My gun's on the ground there. What was I supposed to do?"

I said, "It all happened too fast. Wasn't nothing any of us could do."

Fat-Boy said, "Didn't seem all that fast. He was yelling for a long time."

"It just seemed like a long time," I said. "It was fast."

Fat-Boy said, "But he was-"

"Leave it," Charlie said. "You want to jump in after him, be my guest. Otherwise, shut up."

Fat-Boy got quiet after that. I stayed behind with him while Charlie went to get our horses. I had Fat-Boy pack his bedroll and saddle-up. Astride his horse, with folds of fat hanging in rolls, Fat-Boy looked like a rider carved in wax and left in the hot sun. His horse looked despondent.

I picked up Jimmy's and Fat-Boy's guns from the ground and tucked them in my belt. I gave them to Charlie when he returned with the horses. He examined the guns, declared them both dog-shit and tossed them in the river.

Fat-Boy said, "I paid good money for that."

Charlie said, "If that's true they saw you coming. Besides, maybe Jimmy will get hold of one, shoot his way out of that gator's belly."

His mentioning the alligator brought back the image of Jimmy getting eaten and left me unsettled. We mounted up and rode out. The woods were so dense and the trail so narrow that we had to ride single file with Charlie in the lead and Fat-Boy between us with me leading our mule and Jimmy's horse behind. After a couple of hours, try as I might, I still couldn't calm my shaken nerves.

"That has to be a terrible way to go," I said.

Charlie said, "Well, leastways it happened to a terrible person."

"I don't see how that makes a difference," I said. "I'm talking about the whole of it. A man lives his life thinking he's a man. He knows where he fits in the scheme of things. Good or bad, he knows he's a man. But then at the last, turns out he's nothing but lunch for some critter. As final thoughts go, that's got to be terrible."

Charlie said, "You think too goddamn much. And feeling bad for a low down skunk like Jimmy Thistle is proof. You got a head full of rocks if you believe that little turd had any kind of profound thoughts there at the end. If he could have changed places with you, stuck *your* head in that gator's mouth, he wouldn't have hesitated."

"He's right," Fat-Boy said from the back of his slow-moving horse.

"Nobody asked you," Charlie said.

Fat-Boy said, "I'm just agreeing with you."

Charlie said, "I don't need the likes of you sticking up for me."

"You fellas took his gun," Fat-Boy said. "But you didn't take the knife he had in his boot."

Charlie looked back over his shoulder at Fat-Boy. "The hell you say."

"It's true," Fat-Boy said, and nodded his head. I could tell by the way the fat on the back of his neck moved. "He was jabbering at you, acting the fool, trying to keep you distracted. First chance he got though, he was gonna cut on one of you. People always think. . . thought he was harmless because of his goofy ways and his bug eyes, but down deep he was a cold killer. And really, it wasn't down all that deep. If that gator hadn't gotten him, one or both of you would be dead by now."

"You see there," Charlie said. "That gator saved our lives."

"You don't seem too broke up about your dead friend," I said.

Fat-Boy said, "We rode together, but he wasn't my friend. He hadn't been so kill-happy nobody on that stagecoach would've been shot. Wasn't no reason for it other than meanness. Plus he's the one who talked me into coming to Texas, and that's something I can't forgive."

Things got quiet after that, and we rode along sweating in silence. Fat-Boy and I did anyway. Charlie, despite being dressed in his usual black suit, seemed perfectly comfortable. The weather, hot or cold, never had much effect on Charlie. He was adaptable and at ease in his own skin in a way I could never manage.

We put in a long day of riding, and a slow one too, hobbled as we were by the pace of Fat-Boy's overburdened horse. Charlie tried to make up for it by pushing on longer, but near sundown we were all three too tired to keep on.

We made camp and while I tended to the horses Charlie put a pair of rusty shackles on Fat-Boy's ankles. We usually kept a pair with us, but this was the first time we'd had occasion to use them. I didn't think we needed them. Big as he was, Fat-Boy was slow and noisy, and in my opinion unlikely to make a run for it. Charlie said better safe than sorry, and if it was my intention to start bringing men in alive I better get used to it.

We had a dinner of beans and hard tack, and after the warning we'd received from Jimmy Thistle we only reluctantly shared it with Fat-Boy. We were all three seated around our small campfire. Fat-Boy was on one side, Charlie and me on the other. Fat-Boy cleaned his plate in a heartbeat and asked for more.

Charlie said, "That's all we got."

Fat-Boy said, "There's more beans right there in the pot."

Charlie said, "Go to sleep."

Fat-Boy said, "It's cause'a what Jimmy said, ain't it? I'm a big fat man, so I must smell bad. Is that it?"

Charlie said, "Well, you do smell pretty awful."

Fat-Boy said, "That's cause it's hot as hell out here.

Everybody in Texas smells bad except for you, you no-sweating sonbitch. It was Jimmy had the devil-farts, but he had a way of making everybody else look guilty for his doings. Now I'm probably gonna hang for what he done and I can't even get a second helping of beans. I hate that bastard even more than I hate Texas."

Charlie said, "Don't pretend you're innocent just because you didn't pull the trigger. You robbed that stagecoach same as him."

Fat-Boy said, "Wasn't like that at all. We happened to be there when the stagecoach come along, and Jimmy decided to rob it. We didn't plan it. I'm no angel, that's a fact. But there's things I'll do and things I won't. I only went along to try and keep Jimmy from killing anybody. It didn't work out, but that's what I was doing. You can believe that, or you can kiss my big ass. I don't much care."

I took the pan and set it near Fat-Boy. "Have all you want."

Fat-Boy said, "Put'em in your hat and wear'em." He lay down and put his hat over his eyes. Not more than a minute later he was sound asleep.

I turned to Charlie and he immediately said, "Don't."

I said, "Don't what?"

"Don't start feeling sorry for this lard-ass. He chose his company, and he charted his course. It's too late for him to start lamenting the destination."

"But what if he was telling the truth," I asked. "What if he didn't shoot those people?"

Charlie said, "If he didn't commit that crime he's guilty of a dozen others. This just happens to be the one that'll get him hung. The man has a lifetime of dirty deeds to answer for, and I'm not gonna lose sleep wondering if he's guilty of this one in particular. This right here is why I'm against taking folks in alive. Just complicates matters."

With that, Charlie lay his head back against his saddle there on the ground and tipped his hat down over his face.

I said, "You're a hard man, Charlie."

From beneath his hat Charlie said, "It's a hard god-damn country."

As if in answer Fat-Boy let out a long whistling fart that echoed through the forest. I glanced at Charlie, saw him raise his hat to give me the stink-eye. I turned away from him and went to sleep.

That night I dreamed of dark deep water, and sharp-toothed creatures big enough to swallow a man whole. I awoke at dawn to the sound of Charlie screaming.

THREE

There was light in the sky, but it hadn't worked its way through the trees yet and our camp still lay in thick shadow. I could tell from the sound of Fat-Boy's breathing that he was asleep. A small fire had been started, coffee brewing. Charlie's bedding was still on the ground, but I didn't see Charlie.

I rubbed at my face hard, trying to clear the fog from my brain. I got up, looked around in the morning gloom and spotted Charlie over by the horses. He was bent double, one hand against a tree, and what I had mistaken for a scream was Charlie heaving his dinner into the bushes. After a few seconds Charlie stood upright, one arm across his belly, like it pained him considerable.

"You okay?" I called out.

Charlie turned at the sound of my voice, like he was embarrassed at being caught sick. He walked back to the fire, wobbling unsteadily as he came. He still didn't speak.

I said, "Dinner not agree with you?"

Charlie sat down, said, "I don't know. Felt a little puny when I woke up, then about the time I got the coffee going I had to make a run for the bushes."

I poured a cup of coffee, handed it to Charlie.

"Doing better?"

Charlie nodded. He took the coffee, set it on the ground, then lay down on his side with his knees drawn half-way to his chest.

Charlie said, "Just let me lay here a minute and I'll be good as gold."

I had my doubts about that. Charlie was the sort to dismiss any hurt or illness as a minor annoyance. For him to acknowledge it meant he was in significant pain.

I let Charlie rest while I got us ready to ride. I saddled our horses, including Fat-Boy's, then rummaged our supplies and found our last piece of salt-pork. Charlie didn't want anything to eat, so I finished off the beans and ate half the pork. Lastly, I woke up Fat-Boy, removed his shackles and gave him some hardtack and the other half of the pork. He was grateful and didn't ask where the leftover beans had gone.

It came time to leave and Charlie was still in a bad way. His eyes were sunken, and his face was pale. I had to help him onto his horse, and when he took the reins I saw his hands were shaking. I'd never seen Charlie this bad off, and it troubled me in a way I couldn't quite figure. I said, "You sure you're okay to ride?"

Charlie tilted his hat down to shade his eyes, and made an attempt to sit up straight, square his shoulders.

Charlie said, "Doing fine. Just a little under the weather, but I'm climbing above it now."

Fat-Boy sat on his unhappy horse watching us.

Fat-Boy said, "We can rest here as long as you need. It won't whittle me down any."

Charlie said, "No, sir. Don't want to keep the hang-man waiting."

Fat-Boy hung his head and kept quiet.

Sick as he was, Charlie still insisted on riding in the lead. We had to stop twice in the early going to let him heave some more. As the day wore on he seemed to feel slightly better, although he still rode with that arm pressed against his stomach.

Along about noon it started to rain. A steady, heavy downpour that had us soaked in seconds. Fat-Boy sat looking miserable as he watched Charlie and I put on our rain-slickers. His dark hair was plastered to his head and water dripped steadily from the end of his nose.

Fat-Boy said, "You got any spare gear for me?"

Charlie said, "We do not."

Fat-Boy said, "Shit. Ain't no end to my tribulations."

Charlie said, "They'll end soon enough. With a yank and a snap, I expect."

Fat-Boy turned his eyes to me, and the look on his face made me think of a whipped dog.

The rain didn't let up. In fact it got heavier. The pounding of the rain was a constant, maddening roar, so loud you had to shout to be heard over it. Soon the trail became more of a stream and there were times I thought for sure we had lost it completely.

I said to Fat-Boy, "Why in hell did you and Jimmy

leave the main road to go traipsing through the woods? Where did you think you were going?"

Fat-Boy rode with his head down, looking like four hundred pounds of wet misery. He said, "I was just following Jimmy. He said we were going to meet up with a couple old partners of his. Wouldn't say who. Not sure he even knew we'd left the road. I'm beginning to suspicion Jimmy didn't know what he was doing."

Up ahead I saw Charlie slumped forward in the saddle. He was leaning slightly, and I worried he might fall off his horse. I nudged my horse past Fat-Boy, turning away from the wet leaves and branches that smacked at my face. I got up next to Charlie and took the reins, brought us to a stop.

Charlie looked at me through the curtain of water running from his hat brim and there was no light in his eyes. They were open, but he didn't seem to be awake. After a second of staring blankly he blinked several times and looked around.

Charlie smiled weakly, said, "Think it'll rain."

I said, "It might. Hard to say."

Charlie said, "What time is it?"

"Around three," I said. "We been riding for hours."

Charlie bobbed his head, said "Feels like it. I think I might have dozed off."

I said, "You're looking pretty bad, Charlie. I think maybe we should call it a day."

Charlie shook his head, said, "I got a few more hours in me. Let's push on."

"You're not being sensible," I said. "Let's get you down, let you rest a bit."

Charlie said, "Maybe we should. Just for the horses. They could probably use the rest."

I turned to tell Fat-Boy our plan and stopped. Fat-Boy was gone.

FOUR

Fat-Boy's horse had trampled down a wide swath of brush, so it wasn't hard to spot where he'd left the trail. Between the downpour and talking with Charlie I hadn't heard a thing.

"I'm beginning," I said, "to come around to your way of thinking."

Charlie nodded, said, "Yep. This kind of thing don't happen with dead men."

"It's no wonder he ran off," I said. "All your talk about getting his neck stretched spooked him."

Charlie didn't answer.

Riding through those woods on horseback seemed foolhardy to me. I thought it best to pursue him on foot. Charlie felt the same but insisted on going along, much to my consternation. He dismounted on his own, moving carefully, but steady on his feet for the moment. We led our horses off the trail and tied them and the mule to an overturned tree and set off into the woods.

The path left by Fat-Boy and his horse was easy to follow, but made little sense. It wound around sort of curlicue, unhurried and aimless. Not the route of a man trying to escape the noose. After an hour or so we found his horse, lost and riderless, and looking all the happier for it.

Charlie said, "Sonbitch ain't as dumb as I thought. He led us astray, has us chasing his horse while he goes his merry way."

"How far you think he'll get afoot?"

Charlie shook his head, but didn't answer. He was looking worse than ever, moving slow and careful like an old man. It didn't take much encouragement to get him to ride Fat-Boy's horse on our return.

After we retrieved our own horses and made it back to the trail we found footprints in the mud.

I said, "Fat-Boy."

Charlie said, "Looks like he doubled back. Maybe hoping we left Jimmy's horse behind, thought he could steal it."

"Couldn't find where we'd left them," I said.

Charlie said, "The halfwit's lucky he found the trail."

I heard a sound then, but so muted by the woods and rain I couldn't be sure.

I said, "Was that a gunshot?"

Charlie said, "I didn't hear anything."

We both sat for a minute, waiting for the sound to repeat. When it didn't, we rode on. The travelling went easier. Even with the relentless downpour the absence of Fat-Boy allowed us to pick up the pace significantly.

We followed the footprints along the trail for a little ways, then saw that they veered off into the woods once more. Fat-Boy left a path of trampled brush only slightly smaller than that of his horse.

I told Charlie I was going after him, said he should wait in case Fat-Boy tried the same trick again. Charlie agreed, gratefully it seemed.

I followed Fat-Boy's trail into the overgrown woods once more. I was tired, and wet, and irritated, and I found myself questioning my choice of occupations. I imagined all the jobs that didn't require pursuing wanted criminals through East Texas woods in the pouring rain, and realized I lacked the skill for any of them. Which was why I was out here in the first place. Charlie was right. Sometimes I think too damn much.

Fat-Boy had gone into the woods a ways, then he'd turned and gone parallel to the trail we'd ridden in on. I moved as quickly as I could, figuring for certain I was gaining on him.

I found Fat-Boy just a few minutes later. I saw him up ahead, lying on his stomach in a pool of muddy water. I called his name a couple of times. He didn't answer. I thought at first he was dead, thought the dumbass had got himself drowned. When I got close enough to examine him it was immediately clear that was not the problem. He was dead all right, but not drowned. There was a gaping hole in his back that looked like it was made by a high caliber slug on its way out. Even more disturbing, Fat-Boy's head was gone.

FIVE

"Gone?"

Charlie was staring down at me from horseback, looking confused. He sat hunched forward, and it was clear from his face that he was still in a lot of pain. He considered what I had told him and narrowed his eyes, as if trying to see the matter more clearly.

"Gone," he said again. "Not just shot to pieces, or chewed on like Jimmy was?"

I said, "Gone. As in, somebody cut it off and took it with them. Gone."

Charlie said, "Are you sure it was Fat-Boy? If he didn't have a head it's possible you were mistaken. Or maybe Fat-Boy's pulling a fast one on us."

"You think Fat-Boy ran into some other four hundred pound bastard out here, chopped his head off then swapped clothes with him?"

Charlie thought for a moment, said, "It seems less likely when you say it out loud."

I said, "Because it *is* unlikely. That's Fat-Boy out there all right."

Charlie said, "And somebody skedaddled with his melon."

"They did."

"Why take it with them? You sure it wasn't lying in the bushes somewhere nearby?"

"It wasn't. . ." I stopped to consider. "Okay, you might be right on that one. I admit I didn't look around real careful for his noggin. It was separated from his body, and that was all I needed to know. But if they didn't take it with them, why remove it in the first place? From the looks of that hole in his back, he was dead or close to it before they commenced to chopping."

Charlie said, "I expect we'd have trouble collecting a bounty on just his body."

I said, "Even if we could drag his ass out of the woods- which we can't until we rest the horses and buy better rope than anything we got with us- we'd still have a helluva time convincing any sheriff that it was who we said it was."

Charlie said, "Work better if we had it the other way around. A head and no body."

"It would," I said. "And while you're wishing, why don't you wish for dryer weather."

Charlie said, "If I had a wish to spare I'd wish my gut didn't hurt so damn much. Feels like I swallowed broken glass."

"We can't be far from the main road," I said. "Once we get close we can set up camp, let you get some rest."

Charlie nodded but didn't say anything else. I forked leather and took the lead this time. After a bit the rain stopped, but from the looks of the clouds overhead I didn't have faith that it would hold. I rode faster than was probably comfortable for Charlie. I didn't like the idea of being deep in the woods with a man who took heads as souvenirs, and I wanted to make the main road before dark. The day was fading fast, the sun no more than a hazy slash of light on the horizon, when I saw a flickering glow in the distance.

I called back to Charlie, "You see that?"

Charlie said, "I do."

I said, "Campfire, you reckon?"

Charlie said, "Looks like."

"Could be our head-lopper."

Charlie nodded. "Could be."

I slid one of my ten gauges from its scabbard and rested it across my lap.

I said, "Or it could just be an innocent traveler like us."

Charlie drew one of his Colts.

We looked at one another. Charlie gave me a sharp nod and we rode on slowly. Another couple of minutes and it was full dark. I reined up and Charlie came alongside me.

I said, "You hear that?"

Charlie said, "I think it's somebody singing."

"Not too well, either," I said.

"Downright poorly," Charlie said.

"Maybe it's a defense," I said. "Scare away ferocious critters and roaming head collectors."

Charlie said, "Nope. Just a real bad singer."

Charlie nudged his horse forward, taking the lead once more as we rode on toward the light.

SIX

The singing got worse as we got closer. The singer wasn't just out of tune, he had an ugly rasp of a voice that had likely soured milk, stampeded cattle, and made babies cry. And he was clearly drunk.

The man was sitting on a three-legged stool beside a brightly painted medicine wagon. An empty bottle lay in the grass at his feet. He was a barrel-chested man in shirt sleeves and dark trousers, wearing a gold vest pulled taut around his big belly. He wore a battered top-hat pulled down over a thatch of wild gray hair and a full salt-and-pepper beard. He seemed oblivious to Charlie and me as we rode slowly into the clearing and stopped a few yards away.

One side of the wagon was hinged and the wooden siding was raised and resting on poles to create an awning for the big man to sit under. A coffee pot sat bubbling above red coals in a ring of stone. I could smell the hot coffee all the way across the clearing.

I called out, "Hello the wagon."

The man kept singing.

TIE ME DOWN, TIE ME DOWN

SO I DON'T FLOAT AWAY

I'LL BE HERE TOMORROW

BUT I'M NOT HERE TODAY

TIE ME DOWN, TIE ME DOWN

SO I DON'T FLOAT AWAY

IF THERE'S SOMETHING WORTH HAVING

I MIGHT LIKE TO STAY

I called out a second time but the man still didn't respond. I looked at Charlie and saw him staring at the ground, that dazed expression back on his face. His gun arm hung limp at his side. I gigged my horse forward and Charlie's horse followed along. The motion roused Charlie and he sat up straighter, took in his surroundings. He winced when he realized the singing was still going on.

THE BOYS IN THE BACK

WON'T CUT ME NO SLACK

IT'S ONE AFTER THE OTHER

TILL THERE'S A CRICK IN MY BACK

As we rode closer I noticed a pair of horses in a corral roped off between trees. I could see a door at the back end of the wagon with words painted on it.

DOCTOR HIRAM T. MAXWELL'S HEAVENLY HEALING NECTAR AND ANGELIC APERTIF

"These woods are getting downright crowded," Charlie said. "We got outlaws, bounty hunters, head-takers and now snake-oil salesmen. Wonder what he's doing all the way out here?"

I said, "Maybe he heard you were sick."

The man stopped singing and noticed us at last. He waved at us then leaned forward on his stool to rest his elbows on his knees. He smiled a big, toothy smile that was a bit too gator-like for my comfort.

"Greetings, and good tidings," the man said. "What dark riders hath these fearsome woods delivered upon my doorstep?"

"I'm Owen Ashe," I said. "This is my partner Charlie Brittle."

"Should you have failed to notice the moniker emblazoned upon my wagon, I am Hiram T. Maxwell." The man looked past us at the two horses and pack mule trailing behind.

He said, "Your party appears to have lost a few members along the way."

"Not exactly," I said. "More like we acquired a couple extra horses through misadventure. We were headed for the main road, spotted you here and thought we should announce ourselves."

Hiram said, "Do you gentlemen always announce yourselves with guns in hand?"

Charlie leathered his Colt, said, "In our defense, when we heard all that racket we suspected foul play."

"You are referring to my singing," Hiram said.

"Well, we know that now," Charlie said.

"That particular ditty was of my own composition."

"Not surprised," Charlie said.

"It's called Whore's Lament. It's about a whore."

"You don't say."

I sheathed my ten gauge and dismounted. I helped Charlie down. He leaned heavily on me, one arm around my neck, the other one still pressed tight to his stomach.

Hiram said, "I wrote another one called Drunkard's Lament. It's about a drunkard."

Charlie said, "I suspected as much."

Hiram said, "I don't sing that one often. October doesn't like it."

I said, "Who's October?"

From behind me I heard the familiar sound of a Winchester being cocked, then a voice said, "That'd be me."

SEVEN

"**We walked right into that one,**" Charlie said.

I didn't have anything to add to that, so I stayed quiet.

October moved around to face Charlie and me, keeping the rifle pointed at my head. She was dressed in boots, men's trousers and a dark vest over a chambray shirt. Her hat was black as night and tilted low over her eyes. She looked to be young, I guessed twelve or thirteen, with long brown hair and pale skin.

I said, "What are you folks doing all the way out here?"

October said, "One with the gun asks the questions. A fella looks like he's been to as many rodeos as you ought to know that."

I said, "Was that a remark about my age?"

Charlie said, "I think it was a remark about your looks."

"What's wrong with my looks?"

Charlie said, "They don't bother me any. But women have different standards."

"Women think I look bad?"

Charlie said, "Well, you got those ears. Then there's that nose. Also, you can't shoot worth a damn."

"What's that got to do with my looks."

Charlie said, "Your bad aim takes a toll on your confidence. It shows in the way you walk, the way you sit a horse. Women like a confident man."

October said, "Hey. You two mutton heads are riding my last nerve. Now, tell me who you are before I shoot you both."

I said, "We just told your friend there. Weren't you listening?"

October said, "Brittle and Ashe, I was listening. But I never heard of you. What are you doing out here?"

Charlie said, "We're manhunters." He lifted his arm from his stomach, pointed at his horse, said, "If you look in my saddle bags you'll find papers for the men we've been looking for."

October glanced at our horses, said, "Don't look like you caught anybody."

Charlie said, "It's true. This trip has not been a fruitful endeavor."

October walked over to Charlie's horse and rooted around in his saddle bag and came out with the paper we had on Fat-Boy Barker and Jimmy Thistle. She held them up for Hiram to see, then she nodded toward the wagon.

October said, "Go on have a seat. Help yourself to coffee."

I helped Charlie over and sat him down under the awning with his back against a wagon wheel. Hiram handed us tin cups and poured coffee from the pot.

October sat down on a rock across from us, her Winchester resting across her knees.

In the glow of the fire, and with the rifle away from her face, I got a better look at October and realized she wasn't as young as I'd thought, she was just small. I figured her to be closer to seventeen. The left side of her face was scarred up around her mouth and eye, the skin twisted and lumpy. I'd once met a bare-knuckle brawler with a face like that. It had taken ten years of being pummeled to get his looks to that point.

The right side of October's face was flawless and smooth, so porcelain white it practically glowed. The unmarred side of her face was so delicately beautiful it made the scarred side seem sinful in its proximity, and I instantly felt myself overcome with pity for this young girl.

October raised her rifle by the stock like a club, said, "You keep staring at me and I'm gonna crack your damn skull."

I fixed my gaze on the coffee pot.

Hiram looked at Charlie, said, "You appear to be having some trouble with your guts."

Charlie said, "I'm fine."

Hiram said, "I can see that. When I saw your friend help you off your horse, watched you hobble over to the fire, I said to myself, 'Now there's a man who is in fine health.' How long you been feeling poorly?"

Charlie said, "Came on when I got in earshot of your singing, I'm feeling better now that you stopped.

If the urge to warble comes over you again just give a holler and I'll ride on."

Hiram said, "I learned long ago not to push my assistance on a man who does not want it."

Charlie said, "Apparently not."

Hiram went silent.

With the awning raised the inside of the wagon was exposed, and behind Hiram I could see wooden crates stacked to the roof, each one filled with bottles of his elixir. There was a large wooden barrel lashed to the back end of the wagon. I guessed it held the watered down concoction Hiram used to fill the bottles.

The interior of the wagon was roomier than I would have thought. Even with the crates filling up the front end there was space left over for a small table, a cook stove and two cots. Hiram got up and reached inside between the crates. He rummaged around until he fished out a bottle of bourbon then sat back down on his tiny stool.

Hiram pulled the cork from the bottle and took a long drink. He offered the bottle to Charlie, who refused, then passed it around to October and me. I took a hearty slug and passed it back to Hiram. He took another big drink and held onto the bottle.

I said to October, "You never did say what brought the two of you out this far."

October said, "We're selling Hiram's cure-all."

I said, "To who? Nobody out here for miles."

Hiram said, "Supposed to be a town called

Absolution just a few miles down the road. The rain slowed us down and we decided to stop here."

I said, "First I've heard of this place. I didn't know there were any towns around here."

Hiram said, "Somebody painted a couple of signs along the road that say otherwise. Could that be where your quarry was headed?"

I said, "That would clear a few things up. Fat-Boy said Jimmy was supposed to meet up with some folks, but that he didn't seem to know where he was going."

October said, "So you actually caught up with that pair?"

"Briefly," I said. "Fat-Boy got away from me." I felt that was honest enough. I didn't see any reason to mention he'd later had his head removed. There was no need to alarm anyone.

October said, "What about the other one?"

I said, "A gator got him."

October stared at me for a long moment. "Say again?"

"He got eaten."

October said, "By an alligator."

I nodded.

October glanced at Hiram and swore under her breath. He shrugged.

Hiram said, "I've long believed that when the talk turns to alligators it's a sure sign the conversation has been exhausted. I believe I shall retire. You gentlemen are welcome to share our camp if you like."

October said, "Hold up there. We don't know these men. And I don't like the idea of bedding down with a pair of assholes who stumbled out of the woods."

Hiram said, "This one's too sick to walk, and that one, from what I gather, shoots like a cross-eyed Chinaman. I don't think we're in any danger."

October stood up with her rifle. She climbed up onto the wagon seat, then onto the roof. She called down to Hiram, "I'm keeping watch up here tonight."

Hiram hollered up to her, "What you need to do is get some sleep."

From overhead I heard October say, "Don't tell me what I need, old man."

Hiram said, "There is a good chance the rain will return in the night."

October said, "I won't melt."

I got my and Charlie's bedrolls and spread them out under the awning. Charlie lay down, still holding his stomach, and shrugged off my attempts to help him. When I finally settled in Hiram was still sitting on his stool. Despite having announced his intentions to retire for the night he was apparently determined to finish his bottle first. Exhausted as I was I fell asleep in seconds.

I awoke, once again, to the sound of Charlie screaming.

EIGHT

I came awake quickly. In the early morning light I saw Hiram kneeling over Charlie, pressing on his stomach, Charlie yelling in pain. I started to sit up and was immediately pushed back down by October's boot on my chest.

She stood over me, that Winchester resting across her shoulder.

October said, "Take it easy, dead-eye. He was yelling in his sleep and Hiram's looking him over. Your friend's sick."

Hiram stopped poking at Charlie's stomach and Charlie's yelling stopped. Hiram got to his feet. He looked back and saw October standing on me, motioned for her to get off. When she removed her foot I went and sat beside Charlie.

His face was pale and waxy looking. He had both arms clenched around his middle and his knees drawn up. Worst of all, his face was covered in sweat, so I knew this was serious.

Charlie looked up at me and said, his voice weak, "Just give me a minute, ol' hoss. I'll be ready to ride in a minute."

I said, "That's fine, Charlie. You just rest there."

I got up and approached Hiram. He handed me a cup of last night's coffee and motioned for me to follow him a little ways from the wagon. October watched us for a moment, then went off to tend the horses. She did not appear overly interested in Charlie's well-being.

I said, "What the hell's wrong with him?"

Hiram said, "I should have seen it yesterday, but I was well and truly inebriated by the time you two arrived."

I watched him pull a small flask from his pants pocket and take a nudge. I wondered if he started in this early every day. If so, it was a wonder he could even walk come nightfall.

I said, "Tell me what's wrong with him."

Hiram said, "Most folks call it inflammation of the bowels. What it is though, is his appendix."

I said, "That's what's in his gut?"

Hiram said, "It's an organ. And his has gone bad."

I said, "How do you know this?"

Hiram frowned at me, said, "I'm a doctor. It's written right there on my damn wagon."

"Anybody can paint words on a wagon. You telling me you're the real thing?"

"Real as can be," Hiram said. "Used to be a good one. Harvard taught. Although I haven't done much doctoring since the war."

"So what do we do?"

Hiram said, "He's going to need surgery, no two

ways about it. If he isn't treated soon that appendix of his will burst."

I said, "What will happen then?"

"He'll die in tremendous pain. It's not something you want to see."

"Sounds like it's best," I said, "if I get him back to Beaumont."

Hiram said, "That would be the best thing. But he won't make it. For one, he isn't going to be able to sit a horse. I'm surprised he was able to ride yesterday."

I said, "Charlie's a tough one."

"Well, tough won't do it this time. He can't ride, and even if he could he'd die before he got to Beaumont."

I said, "Can't we haul him in your wagon?"

Hiram shook his head, said, "The road was in bad shape when we came through, probably worse now. We won't be able to get the wagon through until it dries out some. Again, your friend can't afford the wait."

I said, "Then what the hell are you suggesting I do?"

"We put him in the wagon, like you said. Then we push on to Absolution. It can't be more than a couple hours ride. I can work on him there."

"You? No offense intended, and I believe you when you say you're a doctor, but I'm not sure I trust you to go poking around in my friend's innards."

Hiram narrowed his eyes. He said, "Who the hell else have you got willing to do the job?"

I thought for a moment, said, "If you're going to be

the one to cut him open, why not do it here and save him the uncomfortable ride?"

Hiram said, "I prefer to be indoors if possible. Someplace clean, with good light. I've done enough field surgery for one lifetime. If it will make you feel more confident, I shall refrain from imbibing until afterwards."

I took a few seconds to consider the matter. There really didn't seem to be any alternative. Finally I nodded, said, "Absolution it is."

Hiram nodded and we walked back over to the wagon and Charlie. I knelt down beside him.

I said, "We're gonna go for a ride now, pardner. I think it's best if you go in the wagon. Hiram and I will help you inside."

Charlie said, "The hell you will. I can get in a wagon my own damn self."

I looked at Hiram.

Hiram said, "Let the man try. I don't believe his mulishness will last long."

I stayed beside Charlie while he worked himself into a sitting position, his face growing red with pain and exertion. He used my shoulder to steady himself and struggled to his feet. Charlie was mostly silent, only letting a single groan escape at the last as he stood erect.

I handed Charlie his hat and he set it carefully on his head. I stood up beside him and offered my arm. Charlie waved me away and turned toward the wagon. I heard his breath hiss between his lips as he took a step.

He quickly took a second one and stumbled forward and collided with the wooden barrel tied to the wagon. Charlie made a grab for the lip of the barrel as he went down and knocked the lid askew.

When he hit the ground Charlie let out a yell like the one that woke me up. He drew his knees to his chest once more, clutched at his gut, and made no effort to get back up.

Hiram stepped forward, said, "I bet he'll let us help him now."

As I stood there beside Charlie I noticed the barrel lid sitting crooked and lifted it up, meaning to put it back in place. When I did I saw it was full of salt, and something else as well, just under the surface. I brushed aside the top layer and there, staring up at me with the white granules filling his mouth and covering his eyes, was Fat-Boy's head.

NINE

A surprise appearance by a severed head can leave a fella considerably shocked, and I stood frozen for several seconds just staring at Fat-Boy's. Hiram's voice drew my attention away from the barrel.

Hiram said, "That head you see there is not as ominous a portent as you are probably thinking."

I felt my hand settle slowly over the butt of my Colt, as if my arm had a mind of its own. Before I could draw, Hiram produced a 4-barrel Sharp's from his vest pocket, pointed it at my chest.

Hiram said, "No need for that. Just leave that gun right where it is. Besides, I believe it has been firmly established that you couldn't hit water if you shot the bottom out of a boat."

I kept my hand on my gun, said, "At this range, I doubt even I could miss."

Hiram said, "Yes, but you still have to draw. And my hand is already filled."

Charlie said "That goes double for me."

Hiram and I looked down at Charlie. He had both his Colts out and pointed up, directly at Hiram's crotch. He cocked both hammers, his arms trembling from the effort of trying to hold the guns steady.

Charlie, teeth clenched in pain, said, "You're two seconds away from being unmanned."

I heard footsteps behind me, then October said, "And you're two seconds away from being a head in a pickle barrel."

I didn't bother to look behind me. I knew she had that Winchester out and aimed at Charlie. I looked at Hiram and he let out a chuckle that made his round belly bounce.

Hiram said, "This is ridiculous. If October and I wanted you dead, we had all night to kill you. Yet here you are."

I said, "You want some kind of thanks for not murdering us in our sleep?"

Hiram said, "No, I want a chance to explain."

I said, "You want to explain why you have a head in a barrel."

"Heads," Hiram said. "Plural."

I swallowed.

I said, "How many heads you got in there?"

Hiram cocked an eyebrow and looked past my shoulder at October.

I heard her say, "Four counting Fat-Boy."

Hiram said, "It'll all make sense if you just hear me out."

I said, "I find that unlikely. But go ahead."

I took my hand away from my gun. I looked at Charlie and gave him a nod. He hesitated, but finally lowered his arms, put his Colts away. He seemed to sink into himself then, like the effort of drawing his guns had taken everything he had left.

Hiram slipped the pepperbox back in his vest and signaled October to lower her rifle. She did as he asked, but seemed even more reluctant than Charlie. Hiram moved to the front of the wagon, reached under the bench seat and retrieved an oilskin pouch. He opened the pouch and pulled out several documents and handed them to me.

They were "Wanted" notices. There was one for Jimmy Thistle, and one for Fat-Boy. There was a third with a picture of two brothers, both with bug eyes and full beards and the last name of Thistle. I held that last one up for Hiram.

I said, "Any relation to Jimmy."

Hiram said, "They are indeed. Wallace and Wilmer Thistle. Two of the meanest bastards you're ever likely to meet."

I said, "So you're collecting bounties too. That's why you're out here."

October said, "We were following Jimmy when we crossed your trail."

I said, "You're the one's been following us."

I shot an I-told-you-so look at Charlie, but his eyes were closed and it gave me no satisfaction.

Hiram said, "We figured you were trailing Jimmy too, but we couldn't tell if you were hunting him or joining up with him. So we hung back and waited to sort things out."

I said, "Why would you think we were headed to join Jimmy?"

Hiram said, "Before he met his untimely end by way of alligator, Jimmy was on his way to meet up with his brothers. The truth is Wallace and Wilmer always thought he was an idiot. Not sure why they wanted him to rejoin them now, but I'd wager Jimmy killing those folks on the stagecoach was as much about winning their approval as it was about robbery. Anyway, since Jimmy was bringing Fat-Boy along it seemed likely there might be a few other guests invited to the party."

I said, "What about all the rest? The medicine wagon, the heads."

Hiram said, "I was selling my elixir before I partnered with October. I didn't see any reason to stop selling it. Plus, it tends to distract folks from our other line of work."

"Which brings up," I said, "another important question. What would make a young girl like you take up this job?"

October said, "Red Rojack and his gang."

I laughed. Hiram and October stared at me, stone-faced. I stopped laughing.

I said, "I thought that was just a make-believe story folks told their kids. Watch out, or Red Rojack will get you."

October took off her hat, lifted her chin to better show her scarred face.

October said, "Does this look like make-believe?"

Then she spit on the ground, said, "That's all the talk I can handle this early."

She put her hat back on, pulled it low and walked away to finish hitching up the horses.

Hiram watched her go. When he turned back to me there was something in his eyes, a look of sadness, that hadn't been there a moment ago.

I said, "So the Thistle brothers are part of Rojack's gang?"

Hiram said, "They're the last, other than Rojack himself, and he hasn't been seen in years. Word is he's dead."

I said, "What about Fat-Boy?"

Hiram said, "He was just one unlucky bastard. We were following Jimmy hoping he would lead us to his brothers. Fat-Boy happened to be along. When October found him traipsing through the woods alone, she figured Jimmy had slipped away and decided to collect what we could."

"Those other three heads, they members of the Rojack gang too."

Hiram shook his head. "The gang may be her priority, but October isn't one to pass up a bounty, no matter who it is."

I said, "And the heads are easier to tote than bodies."

Hiram said, "Now you're catching on. And the salt preserves them. Keeps their looks fresh enough to be recognized when it comes time to collect."

I couldn't think of any more questions to ask,

leastways none I truly wanted answers to. Hiram and I got Charlie into the wagon without further conversation. Charlie didn't protest when we picked him up. He groaned in pain a couple of times, but otherwise remained silent. We laid him down on one of the cots and he immediately curled himself up again.

I stood over Charlie, recalling how he'd mentioned it would be better if we had Fat-Boy's head instead of his body. October apparently agreed, and it disturbed me to think that she had come to that conclusion long before Charlie.

TEN

Hiram worked his horses hard, pulling the wagon at a decent clip along the muddy road. His haste, I believed, was due to Charlie's condition, and filled me with a sense of urgency. I trailed behind leading the pack mule and string of horses.

The rain started up again not long after we set off, and soon the road was nothing but a swampy mess. Twice the wagon wheels sunk to the axle in mud, and both times my breath caught in my chest, fearing we were stuck. Hiram yelled and cussed at the horses while they snorted and strained until finally the wagon lurched forward and we continued on.

October rode close behind me, and it occurred to me she was boxing me in much the same way Charlie and I had done Fat-Boy. I didn't care for being handled, so I slowed my pace until she grew frustrated enough to ride up alongside me.

I said, "Nice day for a ride."

October glowered at me from beneath the brim of her hat.

I said, "How long have you and Hiram been riding together?"

October said, "What's it to you?"

"Just trying to make conversation," I said.

October said, "Why don't you go jaw at Hiram. He seems to be able to tolerate you better than I do."

"What have you got against Charlie and me," I asked.

"You mean aside from you being a couple of irritating assholes?"

"Yeah," I said. "Aside from that."

"Well, for one thing keeping watch all night deprived me of my sleep."

I said, "How is that our fault?"

"You're the ones I was watching. I don't know you, so I don't trust you."

I said, "I take no responsibility for your mistrustful nature."

October said, "Then try this on. You amateurs cost me a bounty. I would've had Jimmy Thistle's head if you hadn't chased him into the mouth of a gator."

"Trust me when I say we didn't chase him anywhere. The idiot did for himself. And as for the other thing, you took Fat-Boy from Charlie and me, so I'd say we're even."

October said, "Even? Far as I'm concerned both them bounties were mine. By my accounting you owe me."

I shook my head. "You truly are one unpleasant girl."

October said, "We can't all be peaches like you, Alice."

She reached out and flipped up the collar of my rain slicker, sent a trickle of cold water down my back.

Then she rode ahead, leaving me and my string of horses trailing behind. I straightened my collar and decided talking to October was unlikely to be of any benefit to me.

It was mid-morning when we came across the whiskey tent. It was a big tent sitting on a raised wooden platform that kept it several inches off the ground. I knew it was a whiskey tent because of the sign stuck in the ground beside the road that said, 'Whiskey 5 cents. Salesmen not welcome.' Beside the tent was a crude but spacious lean-to for the horses.

"Guess you'll have to stay out in the rain," I said to Hiram and pointed at the sign.

"Let's hope not," Hiram said. "For your friend's sake."

We decided to leave Charlie in the wagon for the moment, and the three of us went inside. The interior of the shebang was roomy, and cleaner than most I'd seen. There was a long wooden table near the back lined with mismatched chairs. There was a crude but sturdy plank bar with a bookcase behind it lined with bottles. The place was empty save for a man seated at a card table, his head down resting on the tabletop. A lantern sat near the man's head, its weak glow fighting against the gloom. The man didn't stir when we entered, probably because the rain pounding on the canvas roof sounded like a stampede. It was a mystery how he could sleep through it.

Hiram said, "Hello, barkeep."

Nothing.

Before Hiram could try again October stepped forward and kicked the underside of the table. The man jerked upright and looked at us in confusion for a brief moment. He was a grizzled looking fella, with sparse patches of unkempt hair on his head and grey stubble on his face. I noticed he wore a boot on one foot and a black shoe on the other.

He rubbed at the side of his face, worked his jaw from side to side. He said, "That's a fine way to wake a fella up."

October said, "It worked, didn't it?"

He said, "Yeah, but you ruined a good dream I was having." He squinted in October's direction. "But I reckon with a face like that you've ruined a lot of dreams."

October said, "That face of yours is no prize-winner, old man."

The man said, "Yeah, but I make up for it with my kind nature. Like not kicking people in the head while they sleep, as a for-instance."

"You wanted to make friends," October said abruptly to Hiram. "You sort this shit out. I'm gonna go tend the horses."

October stomped from the tent and back out into the rain. Hiram and I introduced ourselves. The bar-keep told us his name was Bertram. He didn't ask for October's name.

Hiram said, "We got a hurt man with us. We were

trying to reach Absolution so we can tend to him, but the rain is slowing us down."

"You've done reached it," Bertram said. "Or at least as much of it as there's ever likely to be."

"How's that?" Hiram said.

"Absolution," Bertram said. "This is it."

Hiram said, "I realize visibility is poor in this weather, but not so poor I wouldn't have noticed a town if I were in one."

Bertram said, "Well, there's your confusion. This ain't a town. This is an almost-town."

I said, "You want to clear that up for us?"

Bertram said, "The railroad almost came through here, there were almost some other folks who came and built here, and I made a mad rush to almost have the first saloon here. Then the railroad went elsewhere, as did all them other folks, and now I'm running a whiskey tent with nobody around for days except some crazy hermit lives in the woods and hardly ever buys my whiskey anyhow."

Hiram said, "What about those signs along the road?"

Bertram said, "I painted those in a fit of optimism. I'm better now."

I said, "So this almost goddamn saloon is all there is?"

Bertram said, "Yep. And if you hoped to find a doctor, you're shit out of luck. No *almost* about it."

Hiram said, "I'll be doing the doctoring. We just

need to get our man someplace dry and well lit, so I can work on him. I think your place might just have to do."

Bertram looked at Hiram, then at me. He nodded, said, "I get the feeling I'm not going to have a lot of say in the matter. Might as well bring him on in."

Hiram and I carried Charlie inside and laid him out on the long table. Charlie groaned and trembled while we handled him, but otherwise stayed silent. He fought when I took his gunbelt off so I laid it beside him on the table. That seemed to calm him and he settled back into that feverish, half-sleep state he'd been in for the last several hours.

Bertram watched us go about our business without saying much. As he moved around I observed that he had a peculiar hitch in his step and realized that what I had thought to be a black shoe was actually a wooden leg. Hiram asked him to gather up any mirrors, or shiny pots and pans he might have and Bertram limped off to collect them. He went out the back of the tent, and through the opening I briefly glimpsed a small shack I took for his home.

I watched Hiram probe gently at Charlie's stomach. His hands were shaking badly.

I said, "You sure you're up to this?"

Hiram said, "No."

I said, "That worries me."

Hiram said, "You ought to be worried. This is dangerous business. It's not like setting a broken leg, or sawing off an arm."

I said, "I thought you knew how to do this."

Hiram said, "I know what needs to be done. That's not quite the same as knowing how."

"You've never done it before?"

Hiram said, "Normally I'd open him up and drain the appendix. That's risky enough, but I don't have the equipment. With what I've got, I can cut and I can stitch. So I'm going to have to remove it. And that I haven't done. Don't know if anybody has, to be honest. I read about a French doctor who supposedly did it damn near a hundred years ago. According to what I read the patient lived, and I figure anything a perfumed Frenchman can do, I can do. Of course, it might have been just a story."

I looked at Hiram's shaking hands, said, "Maybe you ought to go ahead and have a nip or three. I think that might be best all the way around."

Hiram didn't argue, just went and fetched a bottle from the bookcase and brought it back. He pulled the cork and took a long drink. He called Charlie's name softly, and when Charlie's eyes fluttered open he urged him to drink too.

Hiram sat at the table and he and Charlie traded drinks. Charlie's were sips while Hiram's were the desperate gulps of a man dying from thirst. It didn't take but a couple minutes to empty the bottle, then Hiram left to go help Bertram.

I sat looking at Charlie and his eyes opened just a bit. He gave me a half-smile.

Charlie said, "Good thing I got such a sunny disposition. Otherwise that sour look on your face might cause me to fret."

I said, "Charlie, you got the disposition of a badger with a toothache. That's on your good days. And this look on my face is just me worrying about our expenses. We're out money on this trip, with nary a bounty one."

Charlie said, "Maybe you can convince that girl to give us Fat-Boy's head. Seems like it rightfully belongs to us."

I said, "It rightfully belongs on Fat-Boy's shoulders. But besides that, I don't think October's going to give it up. And I'm not looking to tangle with her."

Charlie said, "That's okay. Sometimes you don't get the cards you want. Fretting about it won't change the hand you been dealt, you just got to play it and see what happens. But you can't ever fold, Owen. No matter how bad your hand is. Just remember that."

I said, "Okay, Charlie."

Charlie said, "You know I'm not really talking about cards."

I said, "Yeah, Charlie. I know."

Charlie said, "I'm not talking about Fat-Boy, or the bounty either."

I said, "Yeah, I know what you're talking about."

Charlie said, "I'm giving you advice on life. I'm talking about in case I die today."

I said, "Yeah, I got that."

Charlie said, "I was giving you some deep thoughts

to think on. I know you like that sort of thing. If these are my last words I figured it would be good if you remembered them as profound."

There was a catch in my throat as I said, "I'll mostly remember them as irritating. Like everything else that involves you."

"That's okay too, ol' Hoss," Charlie said, and closed his eyes. "That's okay too."

ELEVEN

At Hiram's instruction Bertram pulled the card table over beside Charlie and put what few shiny pots he had on it, along with a small cracked mirror and several spittoons. Next he put the lantern on the table so the reflected light shone on Charlie.

Bertram went off to boil some water to sterilize the instruments in Hiram's field kit and I sat waiting. Hiram sat across from me with Hiram, working on his second bottle, now without any assistance from Charlie.

Looking for anything to take my mind off what was coming I said, "How did you and October get together? Seems odd for a doctor to turn to bounty hunting."

Hiram was silent for so long I thought maybe he wasn't going to answer my question. When he spoke his voice was quiet.

He said, "I had given up on being a doctor when we met. After the war I was generally soured on people altogether. Selling my elixir seemed just right for me. It was an occupation that allowed me to live in a bottle, and avoid folks when my black moods came on.

"That's what I was doing when I met October. Avoiding people. If I'd been sober I would've ridden down and tried to sell her pa a bottle or two, but instead I stopped a ways off, on a hill looking down over their house, decided to sleep it off. That's when Red Rojack and his gang came along. They'd robbed a bank, not realizing it held a mining company payroll. That got the Pinkertons on their trail along with a bigger bounty on their heads than they ever imagined. They were running hard and stealing whatever they needed along the way. October's family had the bad luck to be in their path. That's all it was. Just bad luck for them.

"It was a gunshot that woke me up. Then I heard women screaming. October, her two sisters, her mother. I don't know how long I sat there trying to figure out what to do. It was long enough for the screams to stop. Long enough for me to see Rojack and his men come out of the house, mount up and ride away. Long enough for me to face the fact that I was a goddamn coward. When I finally rode down there I found October standing in her yard with her daddy's Winchester. She'd been beaten, her dress torn off. One eye was swollen shut and the other was blinded from blood, but she took a few shots at me anyway as I came riding up. Her only eleven years old, and already with a spine made of steel. I managed to get the rifle away from her, calmed her down, treated her wounds. The next day we buried her kin and she burned the place to the ground. She's been with me ever since, hungry for revenge.

"Heard the gang disbanded not long after that. There were eight all total, and we've tracked down five of them over the last six years. The Thistle brothers are the only ones left except for Rojack himself, and like I told you, he's either gone to ground or dead. October's determined to keep looking, and I figure helping her is the least I can do. It might not make up for my cowardice, but it has to count for something. Right?"

I said, "I don't see it as cowardice. What else could you do?"

Hiram said, "I could have ridden down there sooner. I could've tried to do something."

I said, "You could've gotten yourself killed. You ought not torment yourself over it."

Hiram said, "If you were me, if you had been the one to sit atop that hill while that girl's family was being murdered? How would you feel about yourself?"

I was silent.

Hiram said, "That's what I thought." He took a long drink.

October came inside and slapped her hat against her leg to knock the water off of it. She looked to be in as bad a mood as when she'd gone out, only wetter. She came over to where Hiram and I were, looked at our collection of pots and spittoons and shook her head.

October said, "This is a waste of time if you ask me."

"Funny thing," I said. "I don't recall asking you."

October said, "Well, I'm telling you anyway. And here's some more advice. If you're smart you'll save your strength for digging a hole, 'cause that's where your friend is headed."

Hiram said, "Your pessimism is not appreciated, girl. Maybe you ought to try and be helpful and get-"

"Nope," October said. "You want to play doctor, you go right ahead. I'll be over here catching some shut-eye."

October dragged a chair to the other side of the room and plopped herself down. She stretched her legs out, leaned back and tilted her hat down. She crossed her arms and went silent, not concerned in the least with Charlie's fate. Within a couple of minutes I could hear her snoring softly.

I said, "That girl is a rough customer."

Hiram said, "She is. That's what comes of a life spent man-hunting and head-lopping. It takes a toll on a person's tender side."

I doubted October had a tender side. From what I'd seen both sides of her were tough as ten-cent steak. I kept my thoughts to myself though. I couldn't see any sense in disagreeing with Hiram just before he stuck his hands into Charlie's innards.

Besides, it wasn't October's callousness that bothered me. It was the fact that she might be right. I'd always assumed Charlie would die by the gun. This was only partly due to the violent nature of our line of work. Mostly it had to do with how Charlie lived. In all the years I'd known him, mortal concerns like sickness and age never seemed to touch Charlie, and foolishly, I'd allowed myself believe it would always be that way. Now I was confronted with the reality that none of us gets to choose how or when our string gets cut.

Bertram came back inside and returned Hiram's kit. He also had a second lantern and set it down next to the other one, noticeably brightening the area.

Hiram said to me, "I need you to go out to the wagon. There's a wooden trunk under my cot. Look inside and get the chloroform and a rag."

I did as he asked and went out into the rain and climbed into the back of Hiram's wagon. The pounding rain was noticeably quieter inside the wagon than in the tent. I took a moment to look around, trying to imagine what it was like travelling in what amounted to a tiny house on wheels. Then I kicked myself for wasting precious time daydreaming while Charlie lay suffering. I pulled the trunk out from under the cot, grabbed the bottle and rag and made my exit. As I left I saw, on the back of the door, a machete hanging from a nail. I tried not to think about its purpose.

Back inside Bertram and I stood beside Hiram and listened as he laid out our duties.

Hiram said, "Owen, I'll need you at the head of the table. You hold his shoulders down, try to keep him still as possible. The chloroform will put him under, but once I start cutting his body will fight. He gets too rambunctious we'll have to tie his arms down. But we're going to keep him in as deep a sleep as possible to reduce that likelihood. Bertram, that's going to be your job."

Hiram pulled the cork on the bottle of chloroform

and doused the rag. He held the rag out for Bertram to take.

Hiram said, "When we begin, you'll want to lay that over his face. Count to six and take it away. If he gets too restless during the operation, or starts to wake up, just put the rag back over his face for a count of three. Leave it on too long and he'll die. Let him move around too much, I nick something I shouldn't, he'll die."

Bertram said, "I'm not seeing many paths through the woods don't lead to this fella's grave."

Hiram said, "There's only one, really. And it's a narrow one." Hiram shot a quick glance at me, then added, "I want to make sure you understand that before we start."

I said, "You seem like you're worried I might hold you accountable if Charlie dies."

Hiram said, "Wouldn't be the first time. Folks like to say God works in mysterious ways. But they only say that when they can't find someone else to blame."

I said, "You don't have to worry. You're not to blame for Charlie's situation. And I don't have much use for Bible ways."

"Well, I do," Bertram said. "And I'll pray for all three of you."

Hiram said, "Fair enough. I'm not opposed to some help from above, long as I'm not the one has to ask for it."

We all looked at one another. It was as if we were waiting for a signal of some kind. Someone to spin the roulette wheel, or fire a gun in the air. The moment hung, no sound but the rain beating down on the tent roof.

Hiram held up a scalpel and it shone like a diamond in the lantern light. In a voice drained of all emotion he said, "Let us begin."

TWELVE

As Bertram counted from one to six I felt Charlie's muscles relax. His brow smoothed out and his jaw went slack. If not for the continued rise and fall of his chest I would have thought he'd died. Bertram removed the rag from Charlie's face and set it an arm's length away to avoid breathing in the chloroform vapors himself.

Hiram began to cut.

I can't say much about what Hiram did, because at the first glimpse of blood I felt myself growing dizzy and averted my eyes. I wouldn't be any use to Charlie if I was passed out on the floor. You may think it strange that I was bothered by Hiram's doctoring, given the alligator chompings and beheadings I'd been so far witness to, but there's a world of difference between seeing violence delivered abruptly to a stranger, and watching a friend being methodically and deliberately cut upon.

Hiram's work took much longer than I'd expected. Thirty minutes, then forty-five passed by and he was still working on Charlie. Throughout it all he gave Betram and me instruction in that quiet, sing-song voice. Telling me to hold Charlie's shoulders down more firmly, asking Bertram to adjust a lantern, or administer more chloroform. I don't know if all of his instructions were needed, or if he was just giving us busy work to steady our nerves.

My neck and back grew stiff standing there hunched over the table. I figured Hiram must be in agony the way his head was craned forward to look inside Charlie. That thought brought on a wave of nausea and I had to take several deep breaths to regain my composure.

Time moved slower than sorghum syrup on a cold plate.

It wasn't until I heard the sound of riders approaching that I realized the rain had stopped. The only sound inside the shebang was our breathing, and some wet noises coming from Hiram's side of the table that I didn't want to think about.

Bertram said, "Sounds like we got some new arrivals."

Hiram said, "Why don't you go greet them. Let them know this might not be the best time to visit." His voice had taken on such a lilting quality I feared he would actually break into song, and that would have killed Charlie for sure.

Hiram's cautious and quiet way of speaking must have had an effect on Bertram, because when he stood up he did so carefully, like he was balancing fine china on his head. He went outside and a moment later I heard voices. First Bertram's, then louder more boisterous ones. Then a particularly loud voice said, "It's a goddamn whiskey tent ain't it? Well, I want some goddamn whiskey."

Two wet, bearded men pushed through the tent flap, followed by a sheepish looking Betram. He gave Hiram and me a shrug as he returned to his place beside Charlie.

The two men had on soggy hats that had seen better days, and both had long, straggly beards plastered wet to their throats. Their clothes were wet and muddy, but it was hard to tell if they were down on their luck, or just having a hard ride of it. One was taller than the other, except for that they were damn near identical. They took their hats off and proceeded to wring them out on the floor. I noticed both of them had eyes bugged out like they'd just gotten a poke in the ass with a cold thumb. There was something familiar about those wet, ugly faces.

The tallest one looked toward Hiram, said, "Whoo-eee. Looky there, Wallace. I thought that ol' bar-dog was shittin' us. They really got a fella laid out."

Wallace said, "Yep, sure do."

I realized then who the new arrivals were. I glanced across the table at Hiram. He nodded very slightly without once looking away from his work.

Hiram said, his voice even softer than before, "I see them. My sole concern at the moment is this gentleman under my hand. All else is distraction."

I appreciated Hiram's dedication, but I had some concerns of my own. Like what would happen if

October woke up. I was under no illusion that she shared Hiram's concern for Charlie's survival, and I feared what would happen if she opened up on the Thistle brothers while he was still under the knife. Somewhere in the back of my mind I wondered just what in hell they were doing here.

While I was considering the variety of possible outcomes to this current situation, two other men entered the tent. They were young, couldn't have been but a few years older than October. They both wore serious expressions, an angry set to their jaws, but it was obvious they were nervous as hell and trying hard to cover. I guessed them for aspiring outlaws. The kind of green-as-frog-shit kids just waiting to be misled by men like the Thistle brothers.

I watched as Wallace looked over the paltry whiskey selection in Bertram's bookcase. The tall one, Wilmer, hooked his thumbs in his pockets and strolled in a wide arc over to Hiram, as if he didn't want to get too close. He bent down to look past Hiram, then made a face and turned back to his brother.

Wilmer said, "Oh, goddamn, that's messy. I only ever seen a fella's guts after I shot him. Thought that was why they was so boogered up in there. Turns out people are nasty inside from the get-go."

Wallace, still trying to decide on his poison, said, "Yep, sure are."

The two younger men stood near Wallace and pretended to survey the rotgut selection. One of them was skinny, and not the natural kind, but the kind that comes from long periods of no eating. His wet clothes fit him like hand-me downs from a scarecrow. The other young man was nervous and twitchy with a face like a rodent. He was as starved looking as the first, and his clothes were ragged and patched, but at least they fit him.

Wilmer said, "Hey Eustace, your pa was a doctor. You ever see anything like this?"

The scarecrow spoke up, said, "Pa was a dentist. He just yanked rotten teeth, but I never saw it. He did tell me he had to cut a man's tongue out once 'cause it was rotten from chewing tobacco. Not sure I believe him though. Pa was a drunk and a liar. Once when I was a kid he told me he farted a bluebird, sent me out to catch it. Had me running around in the woods for hours. Then he beat me bloody with a strop for getting home after dark. No good sonbitch. I ought to have known a man can't fart a bluebird. Stupid damn Eustace."

Everyone went quiet after this, all of us looking at Eustace.

Wilmer said, "Well alright. Now we know that."

Wilmer moved a little closer to Hiram, watched him working.

Wilmer said, "Just what is it ails this poor sonbitch."

Hiram, still using his soft voice, said, "That's not your concern. Now, please step back and leave me to my work."

Wilmer bristled, said, "Talk to me like that, you fat

old bastard? I might just drag you over that table and kick your teeth in."

Hiram stopped his work and froze in place. He turned his head slightly and fixed Wilmer with a cold stare that caused the man to back up several steps.

Hiram said, "Thank you," and returned his attention to Charlie.

Wilmer turned away from us and called to Bertram. "Hey, bar-dog. We're supposed to meet somebody here. Young fella, skinny as these two here. Looks a little like me, only not so damn handsome."

Betram said, "These folks here are the first I've seen in weeks."

Wilmer said, "Goddamn it. I told you Wallace. Jimmy's the same dumb-ass he's always been. Never should've counted on him. Didn't I tell you?"

Wallace said, "Yep, sure did."

Wilmer said, "We drug our feet to give him extra time and he still ain't showed up. I say to hell with Jimmy and let's go on to the meet-up. Big Red has to wait too much longer he's apt to get impatient. And you know how he gets when he's impatient."

"He gets murderous," Wallace said.

Wilmer said, "It wasn't a question, Wallace."

Wallace said, "Oh."

A cold feeling settled in my chest. Were they going to meet Red Rojack? Everything seemed to fall into place with that piece of information. Jimmy had been on his way to meet up with his brothers, anxious to rejoin Rojack's gang. But Jimmy, being the nincompoop that he was, had gotten him and Fat-Boy lost in the woods on the way.

I didn't want to think about how October would react if she knew how close she was to both the Thistle brothers and Rojack. All her time searching and she'd stumbled right into the middle of his gang being reunited. Hot-headed as she was, we were all lucky she was asleep.

I glanced over my shoulder at October sitting in her chair. She was still in the same position, arms still crossed over her chest, still breathing deep and steady. Then she opened her eyes and looked right at me.

THIRTEEN

As October stared at me I gave a slight shake of my head, then nodded down at Charlie. I don't know if she got my meaning, or if she just wasn't ready to make her play, but she stayed in her seat.

Wallace, still over by the whiskey shelf, let out a disgusted sound, like the bottles on display weren't up to his sophisticated tastes. He turned away and left the tent. Eustace and the rat-faced young man followed him out.

Wilmer said, "Hey, where the Hell are you going?"

None of them answered.

Wilmer started to follow them out when October yawned, then raised her arms over her head and stretched. Wilmer glanced her way, stopped and did a double-take as her shirt pulled tight across her chest, revealing her as female to his eyes.

Wilmer said, "Well, shit fire and save matches. I didn't know we had us a filly in here. This party just got a lot more interesting."

October lowered her arms and pushed her hat back, showing her face. Wilmer visibly recoiled.

Wilmer said, "On second thought, cancel that party. You're ugly as bad-luck's asshole."

October said, "You being the expert on assholes."

This gave Wilmer pause. He said, "What did you say to me?"

October said, "I was just saying, you look like a fella who would enjoy inspecting assholes up close and personal."

Wilmer said, "Are you sassin' me, girl? I could come box your ears if that's what you want."

October said, "I'd like to see you try, Wilma. I doubt you could box your own shadow without reinforcements and a nap."

"My name's Wilmer, you she-devil. You best get-"

Right then a holler came from outside. It sounded like Eustace, followed by another voice telling him to shut up.

Whatever Hiram was doing at that moment, he must have been getting to the meat of the matter because Charlie started to groan a little. It was a horrible, ghostly sound that raised gooseflesh on my arms. I could feel his muscles tensing up beneath my sweaty palms.

Hiram said, "A little more chloroform, Bertram. And keep a good grip, Owen." His voice was still soft, but I sensed an urgency in his tone that didn't help my nerves any. Charlie's moaning went on and on.

October cut her eyes toward me once more. I took a quick look behind me, saw her Winchester in the corner beside my ten gauges. I realized then that she hadn't been looking at me at all. She was figuring on whether or not she could get her hands on that rifle before Wilmer cut her down. Since she was still sitting I assumed she'd taken an accounting and decided the odds were against her.

I felt Charlie relax, saw Hiram now had his needle and catgut out.

More yelling came from outside.

October said, "Why don't you go check that out, Wanda? See what's all the commotion."

Wilmer said, "Keep it up, sassy mouth. See what happens."

Wallace called from outside, "Wilmer, you ought come see this."

Wilmer yelled, "Not now, damn it. I got my own business to attend."

October said, "You might go see what he wants. It'll spare you the embarrassment of an ass-whuppin.'"

Wilmer stepped forward and kicked October square in the chest. Her chair toppled backwards and she landed hard on her back. She rolled onto her stomach and lay there sucking air.

I heard Hiram say, "Not yet." I looked and saw he was working his needle with speed.

October got onto her hands and knees, still struggling to catch her breath. Wilmer reared back and kicked her in the side. It was a hard kick, and it threw October onto her back.

Hiram said, "Not quite there."

Wilmer pulled his knife from his belt, said, "When I'm through you'll call those scars you got now your good side." He looked toward Hiram and me. "You two got anything to say about all this?"

Hiram was still stitching. I stared back at Wilmer but didn't speak.

Wilmer said, "Didn't think so."

Behind him, Wallace stepped into the tent with Eustace and Rat-Face right on his heels. Wallace carried something heavy in one hand. He held it up and called out for his brother to look. Wilmer turned.

It was Fat-Boy's head.

Hiram stood up and said, "Now."

Betram dove under the table.

Hiram drew his pepperbox and shot Wilmer in the back. Wilmer gasped, staggered forward and fell to his knees. Hiram's second shot missed and busted a whiskey bottle on the shelf. Then he fired twice more and hit Wilmer in the back again, and once in the ass.

While Hiram was doing his shooting I spun away from the table and grabbed a .10 gauge. I put the shotgun to my shoulder, not bothering to remove the scabbard. Eustace and Wallace rushed outside leaving only Rat-Face.

I hesitated. Rat-Face reached for his gun

I let go with both barrels and blew the end out of the scabbard and most of Rat-Face's head through the tent flap.

Wilmer struggled to his feet and stumbled outside, all the while making a noise like a tea-kettle about to boil over. I figured him for lung-shot, and not likely to get far. I dropped the empty shotgun, went over and took October's arm and helped her back to her chair. She allowed it, but once she was sitting she pulled away like my hand was on fire.

I grabbed my other .10 gauge and rushed outside, passing Fat-Boy's head at the bottom of the steps. Wallace and Eustace were riding away. Wilmer lagged behind, slumped forward, and looking unsteady in the saddle. They were already out of range.

October's pickle barrel lay on its side in the mud. The other heads, withered and blackened, lay half buried in a mound of salt. Those boys had gone looking for some of Hiram's elixir and gotten an ugly surprise. I went back inside the whiskey tent.

October sat clutching her chest. Hiram was kneeling beside her. He was trying to raise her shirt to examine her ribs. She slapped his hands away and said in a pinched voice, "You let them get away."

I said, "Goddamn, woman. I killed one, and Hiram more than likely killed another. And all you can say is I let'em get away."

October said, "That's because you let them get away."

I said, "There's no pleasing you."

"I'd be pleased if you hadn't let them get away."

Hiram said, "You need to be still, let me look at those ribs."

October said, "No time. Those bastards will be half-way to Mexico by the time you're done."

I said, "They aren't headed to Mexico. At least not yet."

October said, "How the Hell can you be so sure?"

"Because," I said. "I know where they're going."

FOURTEEN

I didn't know where they were going. I'd only said that so October would let Hiram look her over. I had an idea where they were headed, but there was a good chance I was wrong. And even if I was right, there was a good chance we wouldn't be able to find them. It all depended on Bertram.

By this time Bertram had crawled out from under the table and was pouring himself a drink with a shaky hand.

I said, "You mentioned a hermit lives nearby. Can you show me where he lives."

Bertram threw his drink back and poured another, said, "Oh, Lordy." He swallowed that drink and said again, "Oh, Lordy."

I said, "I need you to gather yourself. Are you listening?"

Bertram nodded, said, "Sure, sure. I just never been shot at before."

Hiram said, "Never been shot at? I thought you were in the war."

Bertram said, "Not me. No sir."

Hiram said, "Then how did you lose the leg?"

Bertram said, "It's a funny story. I was working on the-"

"We don't got time for any long-winded goddamn stories," October said, and for once I was grateful for her impatience.

I said, "This hermit you told us about? I got a feeling it's Red Rojack. I think the Thistle brothers are going to meet him. They were supposed to meet Jimmy here but that didn't work out."

October said, "That's because you let him get away too."

"He got swallowed by an alligator," I said. "He didn't get away."

October said, "It's the same difference. You lost Jimmy, you lost Fat-Boy, and now you lost the Wilmer brothers. Hell, if I was an outlaw I'd write to the governor and ask him to please put you on my trail."

I ignored October for the moment and focused on Bertram.

I said, "I need you to show me where this hermit lives."

Bertram said, "I can point you in the right direction, but there ain't no way I'm going with you to find Red Rojack."

October said, "If I need your help to find him you'll by God go along."

Bertram said, "I ain't going, and you can't make me."

October said, "You'll do what I say or wish you had."

I didn't like where this was headed.

I said, "Tell us how to get there."

Bertram said, "Go down the road a ways. I'd say it's maybe half a mile. There's a trail that takes you right where you want to go. It's overgrown and hard to spot, so look for a big tree that's got a branch goes right over the road. You can't miss it. If you was to look for the perfect place to hang a man from, that would be it."

Hiram hit a sore spot in examining October's ribs and she hissed like a snake. He declared her bruised but unbroken and she lowered her shirt and stood up. Moving carefully, she went and got her Winchester from the corner.

October said to Bertram, "If I follow your directions and Rojack ain't there, I'm coming back and beating you with your wooden leg."

Bertram said, "That ain't fair. This fella's the one says he lives there, not me."

October said, "Fair enough." She turned to me, said, "If Rojack ain't there, I'm gonna beat you with his wooden leg."

I said, "You'll have plenty of opportunity. I'm going with you."

"The hell you are."

"I can ride with you, or I can follow behind. Either way I'm going."

"I don't need your damn help."

"I disagree."

October turned to Hiram, said, "Tell this sonbitch

it ain't none of his business. Tell'im I ain't some little girl needs protecting."

Hiram said, "It won't matter. He's not going to let you face these bastards injured and alone. Even if it isn't his business. Even if it might get him killed. Do I have you figured right, Owen."

I didn't answer.

Hiram said, "That's settled then. Now I'd best finish sewing up your friend."

I said, "You mean he's just laying there open?"

"I sewed him up enough one of you could've finished the job if I had taken a bullet. But there's quite a bit of stitching to do yet."

I said, "Is he going to make it?"

Hiram said, "If he wakes up I think he'll make it. There is always the possibility of infection, but we'll save that worry for later. I have to say, if he survives, I may have made medical history here today. Not that anyone will ever know."

I said, "Charlie and me will know."

Hiram looked at Charlie and nodded silently. He looked old and tired, his eyes bloodshot and his face haggard. In addition to his fatigue I could see that this matter of his greatest accomplishment going unrecognized weighed on him. Maybe it was just empty pride, but it seemed like something more to me.

I said, "I've always believed that if you're looking to be remembered you're bound for disappointment, because eventually we all run out of witnesses. You have to find satisfaction in the doing. In the end that's all there is."

Hiram said, "That's something to consider. Maybe while I'm having another drink."

October said, "Are you coming or not. I won't wait." She stood near the entrance, holding her Winchester by the barrel, leaning her weight on it like a cane.

I gave Hiram a questioning look.

Hiram said, "Go kill the sonbitches."

Fifteen

Bertram's directions proved accurate. The trail itself was overgrown from lack of use, and would have been hard to spot if not for the hanging tree he had described. It was a bald Cyprus, old and twisted in growth by disease and lightning. One gnarled branch in particular grew straight out across the road. It was low enough that I could almost touch it from horseback, and did indeed look like the perfect place for a hanging, if a man were so inclined.

The trail was on a slight grade and it was narrow and muddy. I led the way, and surprisingly October didn't balk. In fact, she hadn't spoken since we'd left the whiskey tent. She rode leaning forward in her saddle, trying to minimize the jostling of her bruised ribs. Watching the way she sat and her attempt to conceal her pain reminded me of Charlie. There were a lot of things about her that reminded me of Charlie, which struck me as a surprising thing to think about a young woman.

The mud slowed us down and made me nervous. If the rain started up again even this slight grade could prove treacherous. I was also worried about an ambush.

If these men knew we were coming they had the high ground and thus the advantage.

It was while I was having these thoughts that I heard a rider approaching from the opposite direction. When I looked back at October I could tell she'd heard it too. We both looked desperately for a way to get off the trail, but the brush was so dense it would have taken the machete hanging from October's belt to cut a path. Then the horse came into view and I breathed easier seeing it had no rider. I was perplexed, but a mystery was better than a sudden and unexpected gunfight.

The horse was saddled and stopped a couple feet away from me, clearly baffled about what it should do. October and I moved as far to the right as we could, getting poked and scratched by branches in the process. When it finally believed there was enough room to pass, the horse moseyed by us and continued on its way. October and I watched it go before resuming our journey. Neither of us spoke.

A few minutes later I caught a glimpse of a cabin through the foliage. I signaled October and we stopped and listened. Nothing. We rode forward slowly, getting closer and closer to the cabin. We paused again, and still no sound. Finally we broke from the brush and into a small clearing where the cabin sat.

The cabin, made from pine logs, was tiny, not much bigger than Hiram's wagon. There were two horses tied off beside the cabin. Wilmer lay face-down a few feet away. His brother Wallace was on his back in front of the cabin's open door. On the cabin's other side was a pile of freshly chopped firewood.

October and I dismounted. I pulled a .10 gauge from its scabbard and October did the same with her Winchester. I looked at October, but couldn't read her expression. My mouth was dry, and my legs shaky. She didn't seem nervous in the least.

October moved over to where Wilmer lay while I walked slowly toward the open door. When I got close to Wallace I saw his head was turned to an unnatural angle and a bone in his throat poked out under the skin so it looked like he'd swallowed a pencil sideways. He was dead as the Confederate dollar.

October stood up from kneeling over Wilmer and shook her head. He was dead too, which wasn't a surprise given all the holes Hiram had put in him. I was impressed he'd made it this far.

The cabin was so small it didn't take but a glimpse to see it was empty. I stepped inside and looked around. It was almost military in how tidy and organized everything was. There was a shelf for dry-goods in one corner, and a small stack of books beside a straw-stuffed mattress.

When I stepped back outside I heard a sound, like an animal growling. I spun around, hoisting the shotgun to my shoulder. The sound was coming from the other side of the woodpile. I sensed October fall in behind me and we inched forward.

We got right up on the woodpile before I spotted

Eustace on the ground, an ax buried in his shoulder. The blade had cleaved through his collarbone and gone deep. His mouth was full of blood and the noise I'd heard was the sound of him choking.

I moved over beside Eustace, knelt down and lifted his head, let the blood pour from his mouth. His eyes were open and he was looking at me with a frightened expression. He coughed, then groaned at the agony that brought. Finally he drew in a ragged breath.

"What happened here?" I asked.

Eustace moved his lips, but there was no sound.

October said, "Where's Rojack? Is he here?"

Eustace rolled his eyes in her direction but didn't speak.

I said, "Get me some water. I think he needs a drink."

October said, "Get it your own self. This bastard's wasting my time."

She leaned her Winchester against the cabin wall, pulled the machete from her belt and walked away.

I started to move, meaning go fetch my canteen, but Eustace grabbed onto my arm.

In a wet whisper he said, "Big liar. Just…big liar."

I said, "Who? Rojack?"

Eustace said, "No gang. Just a clean house. Should've known. Stupid, damn Eustace."

I could hear October cussing and moving about on the other side of the cabin. A few seconds later she came into sight carrying Wilmer's head. She stopped beside Wallace and set to hacking at him, and with me propping up Eustace he had a clear view of the whole thing.

Eustace said, "What's she doing over there?"

I said, "You don't worry about that. Just tell me where Rojack went."

Eustace, his panic growing, said, "Oh, shit, what's that girl doing?"

October went into the cabin, came out a second later with a potato sack which she proceeded to put the heads in.

Eustace said, "You won't let her do that to me, will you? Say you won't."

I said, "You got any paper on you?"

Eustace furrowed his brow.

"A reward," I said. "Is there a bounty on you?"

Eustace said, "I ain't even done no crimes yet."

I said, "Then your head should be fine where it is."

He started to speak, but gagged as his mouth filled up with blood again. He had another coughing fit, then seemed to relax all over.

Eustace said, "I was gonna be an outlaw. I was gonna be-"

Whatever he was going to be stopped right there. The light went out of Eustace's eyes and he was gone, along with all the bitter memories of strop beatings and farted bluebirds.

October finished tying the potato sack to her saddle-horn and came over to me. She stood with her hands on her hips, impatient.

She said, "He say anything useful? Anything about Rojack?"

"He said he was lied to. And something about a clean house?"

October said, "Why the hell would he care about that?"

"I'm just telling you what he said."

"I only asked for the useful parts."

I said, "It might be useful if I can figure out what he meant."

October said, "Only thing I care about is whether Rojack was here."

I said, "Who the hell do you think did all this, if not him?"

October said, "Just because these assholes were double-crossed don't mean it was him. I got to take your word for that, and your word don't mean spit. Besides, if he was here, where did he go without us seeing him?"

I said, "There are probably more hidden trails like the one we took. And if he's been living in these woods I bet he knows them all."

October said, "Maybe. That's something else I have to take your word for. Leastways I got the two heads I was after, no thanks to you and your sickly friend."

I said, "Did you have to do all that chopping right in front of this fella?"

October said, "He put himself where he is, and he

saw what he saw because of it. There's no sympathy coming from me."

I got up and dusted my knees. October's bloodthirsty nature made me see Charlie in a better light. At least his ruthlessness came from a place of logic, cold and hard as it was. Hers came from an anger so hot it burned anyone who got close.

We mounted up and headed back down the trail with October in the lead. I followed, stringing along the outlaw's remaining two horses. Back out on the main road we found the horse we'd passed on the trail and I added him to my growing string of livestock. I was beginning to think Charlie and I could make more money horse trading than bounty hunting.

It was nearing sundown when we got back to the whiskey tent. It was raining again and the warm glow that showed through the canvas was a welcome sight. I was sick to death of rain and mud. Alligators were pretty low on my list as well.

When we dismounted October said, "It's your turn to tend the horses. I'm going to see how Bertram's set for salt. "

I said, "Fine. But so you know, I'm keeping all these extra horses."

October ignored me and went up the front steps into the tent, carrying her bag of heads and her Winchester.

I led the horses over to the lean-to where the others were, unsaddled them, then decided that they could wait five minutes while I checked on Charlie. I carried my ten-gauge inside the tent, then froze in my muddy tracks.

Hiram sat at the long table asleep with his head on his arms. Charlie still lay atop the table, now with my rain slicker draped over him and covering his face. Charlie wasn't moving. A little further away I saw Bertram. He was lying on his back, but his head was twisted all the way around and facing the floor.

I took several steps forward and caught movement from the corner of my eye. I turned quickly, bringing the shotgun up.

A giant of a man stood facing me from across the room. He looked to be well over six feet tall, barrel-chested with shoulders wide as a church door. He was dressed in a fine dark suit, like something a banker would wear. He was bald on top, with a shoulder-length curtain of gray-flecked red hair surrounding his shiny scalp, and a thick mustache with ends so long they hung below his chin. He held October up in front of him like a shield. She was limp as a rag doll, and looked very small there in his massive arms. I saw the bottle of chloroform sitting at his feet. October's Winchester lay on the floor as well, along with her machete and hat.

Rojack took hold of October's chin with one hand. He pulled her head so her chin was touching her shoulder, showing me he was willing to do to her what he'd done to Bertram and Wallace.

I said, "Let her go, or I'll cut you in half."

Rojack said, "Shoot me, shoot the girl."

We stood like that for several seconds, no one moving.

Rojack said, "Go on and toss that cannon outside. You know you're going to, so stop dragging it out."

The bastard was right. I turned and threw the .10 gauge out into the rain.

SIXTEEN

As soon as the shotgun was out of my hands Rojack dropped October. She hit hard, and I winced at the sound of her head striking the floor.

Rojack drew the big Remington Army on his hip, aimed it right at my face. He pulled back the hammer and my breath caught in my chest. I thought certain my moment was at hand, but then he gestured with the gun.

Rojack said, "Now do the same with that Colt."

I unfastened my gun belt and tossed that through the tent flap.

Rojack said, "Now get one of those chairs there, pull it out in the middle of the floor and sit down. I don't want you in reach of anything."

I did as he said and sat facing him. Rojack kicked October's Winchester and sent it sliding across the floor away from us. He kept that Remington on me as he bent down and picked up her machete. He went to the bar, raised it over his head, and slammed the blade deep into the wood. After that he went and got the chair October had napped in and drug it over a couple feet in front of me. He sat.

Rojack said, "You spooked me when I saw you

outside with that shotgun. Luckily the girl came in first, gave me a chance to get ready for you. Now, you and me are gonna have a little talk."

I said, "What the hell do we have to talk about?"

Rojack said, "You know who I am?"

I nodded.

Rojack said, "Of course you do. I'm famous. Too goddamn famous. That's why I been hiding out in the goddamn woods, to let my fame die down a little before I go back out into the world."

I thought he was overstating his notoriety, but it didn't seem to be a thing to point out right then. I said, "If you're worried about being recognized you might want to shave that crumbcatcher, cut that ugly hair."

Apparently I'd touched a nerve, because as I spoke Rojack's free hand went to his lip, then to his lank hair. He caught himself and put his hand back in his lap.

Rojack said, "That's none of your concern. I want to know how you found me, and who else knows where I am. And remember, that little girl is only alive so long as you're cooperative."

I couldn't see any reason to lie, so I told him the short version of the events that had led Charlie and me to our current situation. I omitted all mention of severed heads and alligators in order to avoid sidetracking the conversation.

After I was finished Rojack said, "I been hiding out in the woods for all this time, and you expect me to believe you manhunters found me by accident?"

I said, "Wouldn't call it an accident. We *were* following the Thistle brothers, and you *did* tell them where to find you. We wouldn't have known about you at all if I hadn't heard them mention your name."

Rojack said, "That figures. This is all their fault. I'm looking to turn over a new leaf, put my old ways behind me and make a fresh start. If those assholes hadn't shot their mouths none of this would be happening."

I said, "So why ask them to come? You were never planning to put the gang back together, were you?"

Rojack said, "No, but I needed those morons to think I was. I'm just too damn famous to go back on the outlaw trail."

I said, "So you came out here, spent your time in the wilderness, and after the gang gets whittled down you call for the last of them."

Rojack said, "That's right. Figured I could get them all together and bring a close to that chapter of my life. Thing is, I didn't expect them to be so damn loose-lipped. I can't have folks knowing I'm still alive. I done too many evil deeds in the past. I don't want to spend my days looking behind me, waiting for somebody like you or that girl to find me. Only way I can feel comfortable going out into the world is if the world don't know about it. Given my famous outlaw status, even a rumor that I'm still around is like to cause every lawman and bounty hunter in the country to come out of the woodwork. I just can't have that."

It was quickly becoming clear to me that this fella's

opinion of himself wasn't tethered to fact. I didn't know if he'd always been this delusional, or if his time in the woods that he kept going on about had softened his head. It seemed that Rojack firmly believed he was just about the most wanted man alive, rather than a half-forgotten outlaw who'd spent the last several years eating squirrels and shitting in the woods.

I said, "Did you kill Charlie?"

Rojack said, "That the fella on the table?"

I nodded.

Rojack said, "Naw, he was dead when I got here. Other one was passed out drunk. Only one I killed so far is Bertram. But I got to cool all of you out now, you understand."

Behind Rojack I saw October's eyes flutter, then open. She slowly turned her head to face me. She was disoriented at first, but I could see awareness gradually creeping in. I looked quickly back at Rojack so as not to give her away.

Rojack said, "I suppose I ought to go ahead and take care of you now. I want you to know, this ain't like the villainy from my old days. I'm just cleaning house. Getting my new life set up. I told the boys that, and now I'm telling you."

I said, "I don't give a damn for your reasons. You're still murdering scum."

Rojack said, "You got me wrong. I did bad things, but I'm making amends."

I looked toward Bertram's body.

"I mean after this," Rojack said. "Once I'm finished up here I'm a new man."

I looked back at Rojack and watched October on the edges of my vision. She was fully conscious now and rolled onto her shoulder and messing with that sack of heads. Luckily the sound of the rain against the tent hid any noises she might have made. I couldn't figure out what she was doing. She couldn't possibly be concerned about a bounty at a time like this. I wanted to scream at her, tell her to make a run for it. But she just kept digging around in that bag.

It seemed the best thing for me to do was keep Rojack talking.

I said, "So how did you get back here before us?"

Rojack said, "Oh, there's all sorts of back trails in these woods if you know how to find them."

I spared an I-told-you-so glance at October, but her back was still to me. It didn't seem like this day was going to provide me with any satisfaction at all.

Rojack said, "I came in through the rear, surprised Bertram. Then I heard the two of you arrive. Caught the girl when she came in, and here we are."

Rojack slapped his knee then, and stood up. He said, "Well, I really do need to finish things now. Should've done it already, but I suppose I needed the talk. I been living out in that cabin for years. Only person I ever spoke to was Bertram once in a great while, and he was no conversationalist. All he ever wanted to talk about was how he almost had a saloon and this was almost a town."

"I heard that one."

Rojack said, "Stayed around much longer you would've heard it a few more times."

All my glances must have given October away, because right then Rojack turned and looked behind him. I knew this would be my only moment, and I took it without giving myself an instant more to consider.

I dove at Rojack and covered the distance between us in a heartbeat. I slammed my shoulder into his stomach, thinking I could knock him to the ground. Instead it was like head-butting a steer. Rojack let out a slight grunt, but otherwise didn't budge. I did manage to knock the gun out of his hand though, and it skittered across the floor and under Bertram's cook stove.

Rojack back-handed me and I tumbled across the floor and slammed into the bar. I scrambled to my feet, took hold of the machete and pulled. And pulled.

It wouldn't budge.

Rojack grabbed me by the neck from behind. His big hand closed tight and his other one settled on the top of my head. I struggled and clawed at his hand but I don't think he even noticed. I pictured Wilbur with that bone poking out of his throat, and Bertram with his backward head, and figured I was next.

October said, "Let him go, you bastard."

Rojack moved his hand from my head to my belt, lifted me up and slammed me straight down on the floor. I saw stars, felt something pop in my left shoulder, heard all the air rush out of my lungs.

I lay there gasping, unable to move. I could see October squaring off with Rojack. She looked like a child facing a full-grown man. October wore a fierce expression and held her hands down by her sides, grasping something. From where I lay I couldn't see what.

October said, "It's been a while, Rosie."

Rojack said, "I don't know you."

October said, "But I know you. And we got unfinished business."

She stepped forward then and I saw what she was holding. She had a head in each hand, fingers twined in Wallace and Wilmer's hair.

Seventeen

Rojack looked at the heads October carried, but appeared largely uninterested. He cut his eyes back to October's face, cocked his head.

Rojack said, "What's this business you say we got?"

October lifted her chin, said, "You're looking at it."

Rojack studied her a moment more. "You telling me I uglied you up like that?"

"And worse."

Rojack laughed, said, "Well, little sister, I just don't recollect you at all. Whatever I did to you, it don't stand out from any other act of wickedness I done. I imagine that's a disappointment to you, me not remembering."

October shook her head, said, "Only thing you need to remember is this. A couple of minutes from now, I'm gonna cut off your goddamn head."

Rojack said, "With what?" He turned and took hold of the machete, wrenched it free from the bar.

In that instant October lunged, swinging Wallace's head in an arc and bringing it down on Rojack's wrist. He yanked his hand back and the machete tumbled to the floor. Rojack backed away, rubbing at his wrist.

October kept her distance, swinging her arms, keeping the two heads in motion. It was a gruesome sight, those slack-jawed faces, their eyes rolled upward, swaying to and fro.

Rojack watched her movements, glanced at the Winchester on the other side of the room. He didn't dare try for it or she would be on him with those heads. And from the way he kept flexing that wrist I could tell October was able to put some power behind those melons. The two circled each other warily in the center of the room.

Rojack said, "All I'm trying to do is start over. Let the past be the past. A man should be able to do that without all this interference."

October said, "Won't be no starting over. You owe too much. And today you pay the freight."

Rojack took a step, made like he was going to grab at October. She fell for it, took a swing with the head in her left hand. Rojack sidestepped, then came back in, sure that he had her. October was ready for him though and brought her right hand around with a backswing and caught Rojack square in the nose.

I heard his nose break from my spot down on the floor. I was trying to work myself into a sitting position but I still hadn't caught my breath, and every movement of my injured shoulder set off sparks in my brain. I thought if I could just get to my feet I could help. I couldn't get to the Winchester, and would be downright useless with the machete. But I remembered placing Charlie's guns beside him just before Hiram's surgery.

If they were still there under the rain-slicker, I thought I might have a chance of reaching them.

Rojack was cursing now, blood flowing freely down his face. He spit on the floor and wiped a sleeve across his upper lip. His breath came in ragged snorts like an angry bull. Whatever amusement he'd originally taken in confronting October was gone. The way his shoulders rolled forward and his chest expanded it gave the impression that his fury was making him larger. October looked smaller than ever facing him down alone.

Using my good arm, I managed to drag myself a couple of feet closer to Charlie. It was slow going. I still couldn't breath very well and feared I'd broken something. I heard a pained sound from October and spared a look back at her.

October had a gash on her forehead, looked like Rojack had caught her a glancing blow across the face. She was backing away from him, shaking her head, blinking her eyes. Rojack moved toward her and she tossed Wallace's head. Rojack caught it instinctively, then tossed it aside. In that moment October gave the second head an upward swing and caught Rojack under the chin.

I saw something fly up out of Rojack's mouth and bounce off the roof of the tent. I thought it was a tooth until it landed, pink and soft, a few feet away from me. It was the tip of his tongue.

Rojack staggered back a few steps. He paused, put

a hand to his mouth, then let out an angry roar. He yelled some things at October then, but I couldn't understand a word of it. In some way it reminded me of Jimmy Thistle's muffled final words, shouted down the gullet of a hungry gator.

Rojack charged at October. She planted her feet and took a mighty swing with the remaining head. Rojack blocked the swing with a forearm and reached out with the other hand, grabbed October by her hair. He pulled her forward, yanked her head down and slammed it into his raised knee. October staggered back and fell to the floor. She lost her grip on the remaining head and it rolled away and came to a stop against the bar.

Rojack knelt down beside her, pressed his knee into her chest and leaned in heavily. I heard October gasp, start choking for air. She clawed at his leg, trying to get him off.

Rojack spoke to her again, and again I couldn't understand a single word of it. Blood sprayed from his mouth in a fine mist, ran down his chin and throat. Finally, when it was clear no one could understand him, he settled for screaming madly as he bore down on October's chest with his full weight.

There was a gunshot, and the bullet slammed into Rojack's back, right between his shoulder-blades. He jerked upright and turned to look at me, an expression of surprise on his face. The next shot hit him square in the chest and he fell backwards onto the floor.

October struggled to sit up and her breathing was a

raw sounding wheeze. She looked in my direction, then past me. I looked over my shoulder and saw Charlie, my rain-slicker still covering the lower half of his face. There was a freshly made hole in the slicker, and the barrel of his Colt showed through. Charlie winked at me, then lay his head back as his gun slipped from his grasp and tumbled off the table to the floor.

October got to her feet with great effort, then went and picked up her machete. She approached Rojack, who I could see was still breathing. She stood over him silently, staring down.

Rojack spoke and this time I understood him. He said, "Wait. Thith ain't right. Wait."

Rojack held up one hand in a feeble attempt to ward off what he knew was coming. October swatted his hand away with the flat of the blade, then raised the machete over her head.

I lay back and stared at the roof of the tent, wishing the pounding of the rain would drown out all the other sounds. It didn't. I heard Rojack scream as October collected what she was owed.

EIGHTEEN

When October managed to rouse Hiram and get some coffee in him, he told us he'd covered Charlie up in case it was the Thistle brothers who came back instead of us. He figured it made Charlie a little safer if they thought he was dead, and I suppose that makes a certain sense if you're fall-down drunk. Which he was.

Hiram set my dislocated shoulder and bandaged my broken ribs. He tried to tend to October but she would have none of it, declaring herself fit as a fiddle and fuck the world. He said Charlie was doing fine.

We spent the next several days recuperating. Hiram and October drug the bodies of Rat Face, Rojack and Bertram out of sight into Bertram's shack. I used my injured shoulder as an excuse not to help. The two of them slept in their wagon, while Charlie and I slept in the tent. When Charlie was healed up enough to travel we loaded him into the wagon, set the shack ablaze and rode back to Beaumont. I felt bad burning Bertram alongside that scum, but none of us were up to digging graves. I figured Bertram would understand, and Charlie said even if he didn't I probably wouldn't hear about it.

October collected handsomely on her salt-cured

bounties. After we sold the horses we'd acquired, including Rojack's which we'd found tethered to a tree back behind the whiskey tent, we had enough to cover our expenses and spend some restful time in a nice hotel. In the end, Charlie and I barely broke even. When Charlie came to me a few weeks later with the papers on a pair of tough customers with a high price on their heads, I was more than agreeable.

As for October, I had hoped that after she'd gotten her revenge she might pursue a different line of work, allow herself a normal life. When I said as much to Charlie he laughed himself to tears, said I was one naïve sonbitch.

As with most things, Charlie was proven right. We eventually encountered October again, and when we did she was still collecting heads and raising hell. When I think of that face, one side dark and twisted, the other light and beautiful, I still want to hope that she'll find her way back to the life she would have had if she'd never crossed paths with Rojack. But then October's own words come back to me, and I know it's not to be. There's no starting over. And sooner or later, we all pay the freight.

Thank you for reading **Guns of October**, the second in the Brittle and Ashe series. If you enjoyed the book please leave a review online. As a bonus, here is the first chapter of **Cold Bullet**, the next Brittle and Ashe adventure.

Cold Bullet
By Timothy Friend
Available May 2021

ONE

Charlie Brittle and I were watching Bump Stewart when he up and vanished before our eyes.

Only a minute prior we'd spotted Bump running across the snowy field in his bright red union suit and bare feet. Charlie signaled me to hold up, and we stopped our horses at the treeline.

Bump saw us about the same time we saw him. He tried to run faster, but only managed to kick up a lot of snow and fall down. He struggled to his feet and trudged on, looking over his shoulder at us, his breath showing in great plumes. He stepped over a slight ridge, and then all at once disappeared. I heard him yell out, then nothing.

Charlie said, "Owen, I believe there's a pond over there, under all that snow."

I said, "Damn, that's got to be cold. Should we go pull him out?"

Charlie sighed. "Beats sitting here freezing."

Bump Stewart was wanted for a long list of crimes across the breadth of Missouri, the most recent being the murder of a dentist who had pulled a tooth before our man was properly drunk. We'd found him holed up in a nearby whore house, but while Charlie and I were explaining ourselves to the owner of the place one of the doves slipped away and tipped him off. Upon hearing of our arrival, Bump jumped out of a window and high-tailed it on foot. Charlie and I had followed him, an easy enough task what with him being barefoot, dressed in red and leaving a path through knee-deep snow that was wide as a buffalo.

We rode down and got as close as we could without stepping on the hidden ice. We could see Bump up to his shoulders in the water, pawing at the snow and ice, trying to pull himself out and having no luck.

Bump saw us and yelled, "Gaaa. Cold."

"What's that you say?" Charlie said. "I can't under-stand you."

I said, "He's telling us he's cold and could use some help."

Charlie said, "Owen here says you're asking for our help. Is that right? Just a minute ago you were trying like hell to get away from us. Now I'm uncertain about my course of action."

Bump, his voice tight and strangled, said, "Freezing. Bastard. Fuck. Help."

Charlie said, "You say this is your weekly bath, and you want some privacy? I guess we'll just mosey along then. Sorry to disturb you."

I said, "Now you're just being mean."

Charlie said, "Suppose I am. That's what he gets for making me chase him."

"Can't blame a fella," I said, "for trying to avoid the hangman."

Charlie said, "To hell with the hangman, it's me he's inconvenienced. But I'll fish him out just to avoid a lecture."

Charlie had some rope, tied one end to his saddle, made a lasso with the other and tossed it to Bump, who had turned a light shade of blue by this point. He managed to get his arms through the rope and Charlie commenced to dragging him out of the pond, and across the ice.

Charlie said, "You might want to find some wood, build a fire. This fella's going to need some fast thawing."

I rode off toward a cluster of trees to look for some fallen branches. It wasn't easy with snow covering everything, but I managed to dig up a few. When my hands got cold and I decided Stump would have to make due with a small fire.

I had just gotten a spark and was feeding it a few twigs when Charlie rode up, dragging a shivering, shaking Bump behind. Charlie eyed my sputtering fire, then looked back at Bump, who had turned from blue to deep purple.

Charlie said, "I don't think that fire's gonna be enough. This fella is done for unless we get him indoors."

I said, "Then it's back to Lady Gracie's, because town is five miles away."

Charlie nodded. "It's the only humane thing."

I thought that about for a second, then said, "You don't care if this owlhoot lives or dies. You wanted to go back to that whorehouse anyway, didn't you?"

Charlie said, "Just shelter from the cold, hoss. And it is awful cold."

It was odd for Charlie to be bothered by the weather. Any weather. Even odder for him to want to dawdle when we had a cash bounty in hand. Unlike Charlie, I was frequently bothered by the weather and always up for some pleasurable dawdling, so I didn't argue. I asked if maybe we should rig up a travois for Bump, but Charlie said no, it was a short ride and the snow was soft.

I probably should have felt bad for Bump, being half-froze and drug through the snow like that. But mostly I was glad we'd captured him without any shooting. The days I don't get shot at are the days I like best. Charlie, on the other hand, likes gunplay the way some folks like cream in their coffee.

The Traveler's Relief Hotel, which was what Lady Gracie called her establishment, was set back off the road, and looked like a well-tended, two story country home. Other than the small sign hanging from the porch awning there was nothing about the place that indicated it was either hotel or whore house.

When we got close a young woman came running outside calling Bump's name. She was wearing a pair of boots and a gown that might as well have been made out of mosquito netting for all it covered. She pulled the rope off Bump and tried to help him to his feet, but he was too weak and cold to stand. They both ended up falling on their asses in the snow. Bump moaned, and the girl began to cry.

Right then Lady Gracie herself stepped outside. Unlike her dove, she'd taken the weather into account before venturing into the cold, and had wrapped herself from head to toe in a heavy fur. Gracie was a petite woman, and the fur trailed behind her. With her pale face and green eyes peering out, it looked for all the world like she'd been swallowed by a bear.

Lady Gracie looked down at the pair sprawled in the snow and called out, "Ache."

A tall, wide-shouldered bull of a man stepped outside. He wore a striped shirt and suspenders, with a bowler hat tugged down low and tight to his brow. He looked to Lady Gracie for instructions and she nodded her head at Bump and the crying dove. Ache took one step off the porch, not even bothering with the stairs, and came over to where Charlie and I were. Standing flat-footed beside me on my horse, we were eye to eye.

Ache bent down and threw Bump over one shoulder, and the shivering young woman over the other. He stood up without so much as a grunt of effort and carried them both back inside. Lady Gracie followed them in.

When they were out of sight Charlie whistled softly. "That is one big sonbitch."

I nodded. "Strong too."

Charlie said, "I foresee trouble from that girl. She ain't gonna be happy when we go to take Bump out of here."

I said, "You're probably right. Although I don't know what she sees in a bow-legged, pot-bellied varmint like him."

Charlie said, "Maybe he's a real sweet talker. Or maybe he can sing like an angel. Or could be his dingus is made of gold. There ain't no accounting for taste."

Lady Gracie came back out onto the porch and said, in her breathy English accent, "Welcome back, gentlemen. When you rushed off so quickly I wasn't sure if we would see you again."

Charlie said, "Wouldn't have had to rush off if your girl hadn't gone yapping."

"You'll have to forgive Goldie," Lady Gracie said. "She thinks she's in love with that scalawag. I'll give her a stern talking to."

Charlie said, "You do that. And make sure she understands we'll be taking him with us soon as he's thawed."

Lady Gracie's eyes narrowed. I could tell she wasn't accustomed to taking orders, and wasn't likely to make a habit of it. With some effort, she relaxed her expression and smiled.

"I hope," she said, "You won't be leaving too soon. Come in and have a drink. It's on the house for all your trouble."

Charlie said, "That's right hospitable of you. Owen and I never say no to a free drink."

I glanced at Charlie, trying to read his expression. He seemed to be taking Lady Gracie's offer at face value. I suspected she wanted something more than to atone for her smitten dove's interference in our business. But suspicious or no, her house was warm and inviting, and our man was already inside sitting by the fire. We hitched our horses and went in, with me feeling the whole time like the fly accepting an invitation from the spider.

COLD BULLET coming May of 2021